DESPERATE MEASURES

A WICKED VILLAINS NOVEL

KATEE ROBERT

TRINKETS AND TALES LLC

❀ Created with Vellum

To everyone out there who prefers the villains to the heroes

ALSO BY KATEE ROBERT

The Island of Ys
Book 1: His Forbidden Desire
Book 2: Her Rival's Touch

The Thalanian Dynasty Series (MMF)
Book 1: Theirs for the Night
Book 2: Forever Theirs
Book 3: Theirs Ever After
Book 4: Their Second Chance

The Kings Series
Book 1: The Last King
Book 2: The Fearless King

The Hidden Sins Series
Book 1: The Devil's Daughter
Book 2: The Hunting Grounds
Book 3: The Surviving Girls

The Make Me Series
Book 1: Make Me Want
Book 2: Make Me Crave
Book 3: Make Me Yours
Book 4: Make Me Need

The O'Malley Series
Book 1: The Marriage Contract

Book 3.5: Seducing Mr. Right

CONTENT WARNING

This book contains depictions of consensual non-consent sex.

CHAPTER 1

JASMINE

*E*ven if I'd been sleeping, the creak of my bedroom door would have startled me into awareness. No one comes into my room at night. Not my father. Certainly none of the men he insists on keeping in our house. Not even the ghost of my poor dead mother dares wander theses halls after hours.

It simply isn't done.

And yet.

My feet ache from hours' worth of pacing, my chest aches worse from the heart pain my father delivered earlier. Another betrayal after a lifetime of them shouldn't be enough to keep sleep from me, but this most recent hurt weighs heavier than most.

He sold me.

Oh, he didn't call it as such. He called it a merger secured by marriage. A meeting of two wealthy families with ties to the criminal underbelly everyone in this mausoleum of a house pretends doesn't exist. I touch my face, the most persistent of my pains, the only one anchored in the physical instead of emotional. When I'd asked him what price his daughter brought, he'd struck me.

My mouth always had gotten me into trouble.

I slip into the deep shadows near my vanity as a man steps through the doorway and into my room. I can't make out his features in the low light, but it doesn't matter. He shouldn't be here. Perhaps my father thinks to send my *betrothed* to ensure I won't protest the marriage.

He'll get what he deserves.

I barely dare to breathe and reach for the letter opener I'd left on my vanity. It is sharp and pretty, and it will serve my purpose as well as anything else.

The man moves on soundless feet toward my bed. If I need further evidence of his intention, I have it. He is no innocent, wandering into the wrong room—though nothing like *that* had ever happened before. He is here for *me*.

I will not go quietly.

I wait until he is several steps past me before I lunge. He's too tall for me to reliably reach his neck from behind, so I go with the next best option. His sharp inhale and perfect still-ness are his only response to the sharp blade pressing against the groin of his slacks. "Good evening, Jasmine."

I freeze. I know that cultured voice, have heard it in both dream and nightmares for the last five years. This man isn't my betrothed, the sword that's hung over my neck since my father's proclamation. No, he is far worse.

Jafar, my father's second-in-command.

I catch myself before I relent. If Jafar hadn't signed the contract himself, he was at least party to it, the trading of my body and soul as they trade in so many other unmentionable commodities. Why had I thought I was special? A princess locked in a tower is only kept away from the world for one reason: it has nothing to do with her safety and everything to do with her perceived *value*.

"I will not go quietly." I don't know why I say the words aloud, why I make this particular claim when so many others crowd my lips. *Don't make me do this. I don't choose this. Help me.* Save *me.* I am a daughter and not a son, so my father will never acknowledge me as heir, and neither will his men. Jafar owes no loyalty to me.

A new word bubbles up, the one I've only ever used in his presence once before. Our secret little game that we've played for five long years, to what end I haven't let myself consider. "Rajah. Jafar, just … please."

My only warning is a slight tension in his body and then he moves. He catches my wrist in a punishing grip and spins to face me, forcing my hand up and out, the letter opener falling from nerveless fingers. He captures my chin roughly, tilting my head back, though I can't read his expression in the darkness. "You want me to save you."

I should have known better.

Humiliation rolls over me, a toxic mix when combined with the fear and anger already bubbling up inside my skin, the emotions too big for this fragile shell of mine. I wish I was larger, more deadly, able to fight back in any real way instead of standing here, shaking in his grasp. "Fuck you."

"Ah, there she is." I don't have to see his mouth clearly to hear the smile in his voice. If the devil exists, he sounds like a satisfied Jafar, all slow grins and carefully curated words that seemed to have meanings within meanings. His thumb brushes my lip, a glancing touch I only notice because I'm so hyper-focused on him.

On how close we stand.

All he has to do is lean down a little …

Or perhaps if I arch my back a little more …

My breasts will brush his chest. And our hips—No, best not to think about that. Not now.

Not ever.

"Let me go," I bite out.

"I don't think so." Instead, he closes the last bit of distance between us, shifting his grip from my chin to the base of my neck, his arm around my back pressing me firmly against him.

Oh my god.

He's so much bigger than he seems from a distance. Not massive like so many of the meatheads my father employs for security. Jafar possesses a lean strength that his expensive suits have hidden up to this point.

And his cock …

He wants me.

A hysterical laugh flies free. "Not so cold and proper now, are you?" I roll my hips against him. I can't help it. It's like some fiery demon has taken possession of my body. Or maybe it's my inevitable fate bearing down on me that makes me fearless in this moment.

Will my buyer want me if I'm tarnished goods?

The thought spurs me on. I roll my body again, an invitation I can't quite put into words. I may be dancing on the edge of daring, but that's too bold, even for me.

He stills me with his hand on my hip, holding me a breath of distance away, his fingers digging roughly into my flesh. "Your father is gone."

I blink. "What?"

"The territory is mine." His grip doesn't tighten, exactly, but it becomes almost possessive. "*You're* mine, Jasmine."

That isn't an answer, but I am helpless to focus on anything but his last sentence. "Over my dead body." I am not some trophy to be passed to the victor in whatever power plays they insist on acting out.

Except …

That's exactly what I am.

"Earlier you said Rajah. You know what that word means to us."

Us. There never was an us, not in any way that could be quantified. Barbed words exchanged time and time again, each of us seeking to dig deeper, to incite a response, to push past the icy surface layer and bring forth irritation, anger, frustration. *Something.*

Words. It was only ever words.

Tonight is the first time Jafar has ever touched me.

I shiver at the thought. "It means you stop." I'm not even sure where that truth originates. I've only had cause to use it once, the only time Jafar's cutting remarks strayed too close to causing me harm. A single word and he immediately retreated; his dark eyes grave. We never spoke of it again.

"It means I stop," he agrees.

There it is again, the softest touch of his thumb sliding down the side of my neck. So faint I might have imagined it. I lick my lips, and I swear I can actually *feel* his attention sharpening on my mouth.

He shakes his head. "Everything that was your father's is now mine. Everything, Jasmine."

"Including me," I say the words, hating them. Hating *him* in this moment for reminding me of my role in all this. Not an active participant. Never that.

"Including you," he says softly. Again, I hear more than see his smile. "However, I'm feeling remarkably charitable tonight. This is your chance at that freedom you claim to want so badly. Say the word and walk out the door. None of my men will touch you. No one will chase you down. You'll never hear from me or mine again."

My breath stalls in my lungs. *Freedom.* It's a trap. It *must* be a trap. I am Jasmine Sarraf, and I am as close to royalty as there comes in this city. I have an inheritance waiting for my thirtieth birthday—or my marriage—that would make kings weep with envy.

My inheritance.

The door of the trap springs shut behind me with a click I can almost hear. "If I leave, you'll take my money."

"On the contrary. It's *my* money now."

"Thief."

"I can hardly steal what I won by might. Your father made his choices. They were the wrong ones, and he's lost everything as a result." He leans closer, bringing with him the scent of his spicy aftershave. "Choose, Jasmine."

As if there is a real choice. I am a twenty-five-year-old woman who's never left my father's extensive grounds. My only real-world experience centers around throwing parties and playing to expectations, allowing people to see my pretty face without concerning themselves with my mind, my ambitions, *me*. I've never had a job. I have a diploma, but I let my father put off my arguments for attending college. Just like I let him shout down my ambitions and plans to carve out a space for my plans to make our organization stronger. Every single connection I have will turn their back on me if I can no longer wield the money and power the Sarraf name means.

Or used to mean.

Jafar's coup will ensure my father's allies turn their backs on me even if I have access to my trust fund.

It takes every bit of courage I have to lift my chin, to banish any quiver from my tone. "Give me my money, Jafar. I won't challenge you. I'll leave and you'll never see me again."

He laughs. The bastard *laughs* at me, the sound filling the room and taking up far too much space. "You want to have it all without consequences. That's not how this works, and you know it." Another of those laughs that has me fighting not to curl my toes against the thick carpet beneath my feet.

Jafar releases me so quickly, I almost fall without his touch to fight against. "I'll make you a deal, Jasmine."

Another trap.

That's why my heartbeat kicks into high gear, a stampede of one in my chest. Fear. Understandable and justifiable, considering my circumstances. It's certainly not something akin to delight at the opportunity to pick up whatever gauntlet he's about to throw at my feet.

Jafar moves away, his features still hidden from me in the darkness. As if I don't have them memorized, from his close-cropped black curling hair, to his medium brown skin that darkens over the summer months, to his perfectly groomed beard. And those eyes. Those dark eyes *haunt* me.

He stops near my bed, and I would give a fortune to know his thoughts as he looks down at the tangled sheets where I spend every night. Finally, he turns to face me. "Run, Jasmine. If you make it to the front door, I'll release you, trust fund intact."

Run.

I plant my feet. "And if I don't?"

Another of those sinful chuckles. "Then you're mine, body and soul."

A thrill cascades through me, intense enough to steal my breath. *His.*

No. I give myself a shake. No, no, *no.*

I've fought a losing battle from the time I first realized my place in my father's business, fought to be considered an actual person instead of an asset. Since I realized that my body and looks are more important than anything my brain can accomplish. If my father truly is gone, that means I have a chance to set a new course.

But only if I make the right move tonight.

I part my lips, the word that would set me free tingling against my tongue. *Rajah.* That's what I should want, isn't it?

To be gone from this place and this man and all the strings attached to what he's offering me. Just another kind of ownership.

You're mine, body and soul.

No misunderstanding his meaning.

If he catches me …

I shouldn't want him to catch me.

With a shaking breath, I put away my desires. They betray me the same way this man betrayed my father. Deserving or not, it *is* a betrayal. I pull my robe more firmly around me, a laughably worthless action considering how short and silky it is. The slick fabric reveals more than it conceals, and if I wonder if the shadows blind Jafar the same way they do to me, his nearly soundless inhale at my movement tells me—he can see me enough to want me.

But then, he's always watched me with a hot gaze beneath those hooded eyes.

And me? I enjoyed the attention. The thrill of it, of how forbidden it was to be desired by *this* man.

More the fool I was. He's just as bad as my father. Worse, in some ways, because while my father had many faults, breaking his word was never one of them. For better or worse, when he said he'd do a thing, he followed through on it.

Jafar promised my father his loyalty.

Look where that's left us.

I take a step back, and then another. A third brings me flush with the door. "I will walk out that door with my money *and* my freedom."

"Then run, Jasmine. I'm feeling generous, so I'll even give you to the count of ten."

Generous? Never. More like he wants to draw this out, to give me a moment where I can actually taste victory before he snatches it away. This is all a game to him. *Everything* seems to be a game to Jafar.

I don't hesitate this time. I throw open the door and flee down the hall, my bare feet slapping the cold tile in time with my racing heart. The front door never felt so far away. Three staircases, half a dozen halls, more rooms than I care to count. All of it stands between me and my freedom.

If you really wanted freedom, you should have used your safe word.

I ignore the sensible voice whispering through me. Freedom without resources is no freedom at all. This is the only way.

I reach the stairs as my bedroom door opens behind me. Even though I know better, I look over my shoulder as Jafar steps into the hall and adjusts the cuffs of his suit jacket. God, he's magnificent. Evil and manipulative, and far too attractive for my peace of mind. Our gazes collide over the distance and the slow curve of his lips into a satisfied grin nearly sends me falling down the stairs.

He starts toward me.

I flee for my life.

CHAPTER 2

JASMINE

I sprint faster than I've ever run before. Down staircase after staircase, flying around the corners with enough momentum that my long hair kisses the wall at every turn. I know before I hit the ground level that I won't be fast enough. That I've made it this far is only because Jafar enjoys the chase. I know that, but I can't stop myself from trying to win against the odds stacked against me.

Freedom, true freedom, waits.

Entrapment bites at my heels.

I know he expects me to take the main route to the front door, a wide hallway that cuts nearly the length of my father's house. It's meant to showcase his wealth, the walls lined with priceless works of art and each open doorway giving glimpses of rooms filled with more of the same. This is where my father brings people when he wants to impress them, intimidate them, influence them.

Or at least he used to.

I can't think about that now.

I swing around the corner and race through the second

door down the hall. If I can lose Jafar in the maze of rooms populating the floor plan, I might have an actual chance.

The thought barely forms in my mind when a weight hits my back hard enough to take me to the floor. I shriek and throw my hands out, but Jafar is already rolling us, taking the brunt of the impact. The temptation to go limp, to give in, to not make this a fight, rises.

Fuck that.

I elbow him with everything I've got, and his quiet *oomph* is music to my ears. His grip goes slack for half a second, and that's all I need to slither out of the cage he's made his body. I almost make it. He catches me around my hips and flips me onto my back.

And then he's there, where I've dreaded and desired him, between my thighs, pinning my hips to the ground with his weight, his hands bracketing my wrists in a bruising grip. Overpowering me so easily, he's not even breathing hard. I loathe him so much in that moment, I arch up and try to headbutt him. All that does is draw a low rumble of a laugh from his throat. "Brat."

"I hate you."

"Do you?"

How can he lie here and talk to me as if we're having any other conversation in any other circumstance? I can't catch my breath, can't think past the hard length of his cock pressed against me, past his heavy weight holding me down. "Let me go."

"No." He transfers both my wrists to one of his hands and forces my arms over my head. I fight him. Of course I fight him. But the thrashing only loosens my robe, the silk sliding across my bare breasts and exposing me. Jafar glances down and his mouth goes hard. He uses his free hand to clasp my chin, stilling me. "Last chance, Jasmine."

I know what he wants to hear.

If I had any self-preservation, I'd give him the word that would stop everything. For reasons I refuse to examine, I won't. I have lost so much in the last few months. I can't lose any more. I *won't*.

I wrench my chin out of his grip and bite his thumb. Hard. He doesn't wince. To show even that much reaction would be too much for Jafar. He just leans away enough to flip me back onto my stomach before his weight pins me in place again. I fight, but I might as well rail against a hurricane. I'm helpless as he maneuvers my legs farther apart and grips my throat, arching me back until I'm looking down the hallway we lay in the middle of. His beard scrapes against my neck and then I feel his teeth against the sensitive skin there. "Scream if it makes you feel better. We both know why you won't make me stop. You want this."

"I don't want this." I *might* want this.

One of his hands snakes between my stomach and the floor, working ever southward. "Shall we see about that?"

I thrash, but he's got me too effectively pinned. Humiliation heats my face. I know what he'll find even before his fingers slip beneath the band of my silk panties and lower yet. The truth of me. Hot and wet and aching to be filled by *him*.

No.

No, damn it, I shouldn't want this.

But a whimper still escapes my lips when he pushes a single finger into me. How many times have I imagined being touched like this? A thousand? A hundred thousand? More. It's not the same when it's my fingers driving me to new heights. I'm too soft, too tentative, too *me*.

Jafar is none of those things. He touches me like he's known my body before. Like maybe he's imagined this, too.

He doesn't give me the chance to get over the shock of him

doing this *here*. In the middle of the hallway where I can hear low male voices not too far away. Does he think to defile me in my father's house? Right on the floor like a pair of animals?

He withdraws his hand and holds his finger in front of my face, wet with my traitorous desire. "Tell me again how you don't want this."

Time and time again, stretching back through my entire life, I have bent instead of standing my ground. Every. Single. Time. If I was smart, I'd do it this time, too. He tenses against my back, his body filled with the promise of violence and more. Would he be gentle with me if I conceded, if I admitted just how much I want this?

I'll never know. "I don't want this." Even as my mouth forms the words, my hips lift against his, the slightest undulation to betray me.

Jafar curses. "Stubborn until the bitter end." He shoves up my robe and shifts his grip to the back of my neck, pushing my face against the cool tile of the floor. A rip and then my panties are gone, tossed against the wall in my line of sight. Discarded and forgotten.

I'll be damned before I join them.

I struggle, fighting to turn over. When he keeps me pinned, words fly free. "You do this, you better look me in the fucking eyes while you do it."

Jafar, the bastard, laughs. "Did you think you had a say? You don't." He uses his thighs to spread my legs obscenely and then he palms me again, spearing me with one finger and then two. "What a treacherous daughter you are, wet and panting on the floor of your father's house, riding the fingers of the man who took everything from him."

He's right, but I can't quite gain control of my hips. His fingers feel so incredible inside me, but he doesn't drive them deep like I crave. He's cruel in his gentleness, in the slow touch while he holds me in this vulgar position so effortlessly.

"I hate you," I gasp. "I don't want this." Pleasure coils through me, tighter and tighter, centering on my clit and the slow circling of his thumb there. I press my fingers hard against the tile, desperate for more leverage to force him to finish this. So close.

His hand drops away and then his voice is in my ear, low and rougher than I've ever heard it. "Repeat it enough, and it might even be true." He lost his cultured facade somewhere along the way, and I'd give anything to be able to see the look on his face right now. The sound of his zipper dragging down seems to echo unnaturally loud against our harsh breathing. And then his cock is there, pressing at my entrance.

I tense, waiting, hoping, that he'll drive it deep.

Nothing. Nothing but the threat of him.

The promise of him.

He's giving me one last chance, I realize. One last chance to change my mind, to be anything other than what I am. Easier to pretend I fought this, to say over and over again that I didn't want it. My body knows the truth. My mind does, too.

I was never that good at lying to myself.

I can't move my hips in my current position, my legs spread and ass lifted. I don't have to. I have the best weapon in the world. "What are you waiting for, Jafar? Lost your nerve?" I swallow hard, but my voice still comes out just as ragged as his. "We both know I can't make you stop. I *won't* make you stop."

He goes still for one eternal moment. I have the hysterical thought that he's going to make me beg, to put my betrayal into words the same way I've put it into action.

And then he grips my hip and shoves deep. I scream. I

can't help it. I might be a virgin only in the most technical sense—that I've never had a man inside me—but any physical evidence of it is long gone thanks to the illicit sex toys I secreted into my room years ago.

It doesn't seem to matter. He's big, bigger than anything I've played with to date, and he's not giving me time to adjust. Jafar pulls out and shoves back in, hard enough to move me several inches up the hallway despite his hold on my neck. The tile bites my knees and my hands slap the floor, sounds slipping from my lips that are more animal than woman. It hurts. Everything hurts. But I can't stop arching back against him as much as I'm able, the pain twining with pleasure that I have no way to describe.

The earlier denied orgasm rolls over me, and my breathless cries morph into a single word. His name. A benediction and a curse. Over and over and over again. "Jafar, Jafar, *Jafar.*"

He keeps thrusting, his low sounds just as animal-like as mine. At last moment, he pulls out of me and something hot and thick lands across my ass and upper thighs.

My body morphs into something less solid than muscle and bone. I drop to the ground. I can do nothing but lay there and relearn how to breathe with my lower half exposed, his come cooling on my bare skin.

He just …

That bastard just …

"Say it, Jasmine."

I blink rapidly, mind gone hazy and indistinct with the shocking combination of pleasure and pain he'd delivered, the dose of humiliation and possession that he cultivated like fine wine. I lick my lips, and it takes me two tries to form the words. "Say what?"

"Say 'Thank you, Jafar.'"

Over my dead body. "The hell I will."

"Disobedient to the very end." His chuckle has my body

clenching despite my rage. "We'll work on it." He moves off me, and a few moments later he catches me under my arms and pulls me to my feet and turns me to face him. My knees buckle, the traitors. I'm forced to grab his shoulders to stay upright.

It's right around then that we get our first good look at each other.

There's no evidence of what we just did on his face. It might be there in the extra growl in his voice, but he appears as composed and distant as ever. It makes me want to strike him. My world just came crashing down around me, and even without access to a mirror, I know that I look a mess.

Jafar skims off my robe, ignoring my weak attempt to cover my breasts. He uses the wadded-up fabric to clean the evidence of himself from my ass and thighs, and somehow that's the most humiliating part of this whole experience. "I can do it."

"No." Just that. Nothing more. He tosses the ruined fabric to join my panties on the floor and only then does he look at my face. At the bruise darkening my skin, courtesy of my father's hand. Storm clouds gather in his dark eyes. He touches my chin, tilting my face to the side. "Did he do this?"

"You're going to have to be more specific." When he just waits, I relent. I'm too tired for this ridiculous argument. Too confused and exhilarated and depressed, all at once. "My father doesn't like it when I talk back."

"You always talk back. He's never hit you before."

"Hasn't he?"

His mouth goes tight and I have the presence of mind to wonder if my father is still among the living. He may not stay that way for long with the fury emanating from Jafar.

Funny that he wasn't angry until this point.

He unbuttons his shirt in neat, precise movements and

shrugs out of it. I skitter back a step. "My room is upstairs. I'll get my own clothes."

"You know better."

Damn it, but I do.

This is as much about a power play as it is about anything as mundane as lust. Jafar might want me, but it's not simply because he's a man who wants a woman. I am a symbol, an indicator that his victory over my father is complete on every level. Power, money, home, daughter.

Likely in that order.

Jafar pulls his shirt on me and buttons it up as if he dresses me in his clothing regularly. I'm tall enough that it barely covers my ass, but apparently that isn't the point.

The conqueror must parade his stolen goods in front of his men.

"Why not just throw a collar on my neck and lead me around naked to really seal my degradation?"

His lips curve. "Maybe another time." He brushes my hair back and then his finger is there, tracing the shape of the bruises coloring my cheekbone. Marking it. Memorizing it.

Yes, if my father is alive, he'll come to regret that strike. I have no doubts about that.

"You're in my world now, Jasmine."

Was that supposed to comfort me? He's a snake in the garden, tempting me into delicious sin and then abandoning me in every way that counted once the deed is done. Jafar doesn't seem to need a response. He simply tosses me over his shoulder like some old-world war prize. I want to scream and curse and flail, but it's only his upper arm across the bottom of my ass that holds his shirt in place. If I fight him, I won't get free, and everyone will see every part of me.

Just more humiliation.

"You'll pay for this."

"Unlikely." He starts down the hallway with an easy

stride, as if my weight on his shoulder is completely inconsequential. As if I'm nothing more than another token of his superiority.

I'm thankful that my long hair hides my face as we leave the hallway and enter the main foyer. It's a ridiculously overdrawn room with two curving staircases leading up to the second floor and more than enough space for fifty people to stand comfortably.

It sounds as if it's filled to capacity.

A murmur goes through the people gathered. It's speculative and filled with no small amount of gleeful malice. They think Jafar raped me, that he took by force something they followed with covetous eyes since the time I hit puberty and developed breasts.

They could never comprehend the level of my betrayal, that I wanted him to defile me the way he did, that I welcomed his touch even as I mouthed all the protests I could muster. Every word but the one that would make a difference.

Jafar knows.

He owns me, and I have no one to blame but myself.

"Well done." His voice booms out, silencing everyone. "Tonight is for celebrating." He lets them cheer, lets the ugliness of their glee wash over me. "Tomorrow, we get to work."

"Where you taking the girl, boss?" A voice from the crowd. I know that voice. It's Richard, a man who served on my personal protective detail despite my begging my father to remove him. Another fight I lost. He laughed, the sound buoyed by others around him. "Share the spoils of war!"

Share *me*.

I tense. I can't help it.

Surely he wouldn't …

Jafar goes still. I sense the danger before the rest of the room. But then, I've spent an inordinate amount of time studying him over the years. He *always* goes still before he cuts someone off at the knees. "Richard, would you come into my home and steal from me?"

Stammering. Richard realizes his mistake. I could tell him it's too late, but instead I squeeze my eyes shut, wanting this whole spectacle to be over.

"This woman is mine, by right and by might. Touch her, and I will crush you."

"She's just a pair of tits, boss." This from farther away, deeper in the crowd as if that will save them.

"Touch her, and I will crush you," he repeats.

Jafar turns and pushes through the doors. I can't maintain the tension in my body any longer, and I slump down against him. "I hate you." Maybe if I say it enough times, it will even morph into the truth.

Anything is possible.

He moves down the steps, and even in my fury and fear, I notice that he takes pains to keep his stride even and not jar me more than necessary. I can't bring myself to feel grateful. Not after the events of the last hour. Not after his men were so painfully clear of what they would have done to me—what they *wanted* to do to me.

I shudder. "I'm going to be sick."

Instantly, he has my feet on the ground and guides me to a bench situated near the driveway. "Head down between your knees." His big palm on my upper back doesn't give me a choice in the placement. It helps. I hate that it helps. "They wanted to—"

"No one will touch you."

"You did."

It's only when his hand stops rubbing on my back that I realize it was in motion to begin with. I expect him to argue that I wanted everything he did to me and more. To point out that we have one foolproof brake when it comes to our rules of engagement and I didn't enact it.

I should know better by now.

"I did more than touch you. I held you down and shoved my cock into that tight little cunt of yours, and even while you cursed me, you came harder than you've ever come before. " His breath ghosts against the shell of my ear. "I'm going to do it again. And again. And again. You made your choice, Jasmine. Now you have to live with it."

CHAPTER 3

JAFAR

Five years of maintaining perfect control and I've thrown it away in a single night. Anyone else would call the events of the last few hours a complete and utter victory. I look at the woman curled up on the seat next to me, her long legs tucked under the shirt that I put on her. Jasmine will wear my bruises in the morning, marks on her hips from my fingers and marks on her knees from the marble floor. That doesn't concern me. She made her choice with eyes wide open, and I'm a bastard because I look forward to every single power struggle in the future spinning out between us.

Connected.

Forever.

She's mine now the same way her father's fortune and business and allies are now mine.

My gaze tracks the curve of the bruise darkening her cheekbone. It's not particularly brutal as bruises go, but what it represents has an inferno of fury spiraling up through me. That fucker kept her in a cage, playing the doting father when it served his purposes, and sold her to that little shit of an upstart. Then he had the audacity to strike her when she protested?

I'm no better than he is in so many ways, but when I strike a woman, it's because she damn well wants it. Because she gets off on it. Balthazar Sarraf hit his daughter the same way a man kicks a dog because it didn't immediately follow his orders.

It's a shame he's already dead, because I would happily kill him for this sin alone.

"Stop staring at me."

I ask the thing I should have thought about before shoving my cock into her. "Are you on birth control?"

She shoots me a surprised look. "Of course. I have an IUD."

Of course. As if it's a given. "How did you manage that?"

"Our family doctor likes bribes and hates my father. It only took one of my mother's heirloom pieces to convince him to give me one." She runs her fingers through her hair almost absently. "I don't have control of so many things—of *anything*—but I ensured I'd at least have control of whether or not I have children."

Jasmine always was more savvy than her father gave her credit for. She's managed to work around him at least a dozen times since I joined the organization, and those are just the ones I noticed.

"I'm tested regularly," I finally say. "You have nothing to worry about from me on that front."

"That's good. I have to worry about you on every other front." She turns and stares out the window. She doesn't look away as we drive into town and the city creeps up around us.

It strikes me that she's never seen any of this before. Sarraf kept expansive and immaculate grounds surrounded by a truly impressive wall and security system. He may have traveled extensively, but his daughter had been confined to the property. For her safety, of course.

To keep her under his thumb, more like.

I have no high horse to stand on when it comes to that. I want Jasmine confined, too. My collar on her neck, its chain never far from my hand. I want her on her knees in subservience. I want to fucking *ruin* her.

If there's a good guy in this scenario, it's not my part to play.

I let the silence drag out as we pass through the streets. This time of night Carver City is far from empty, but the traffic that plagues the streets during rush hour is long gone. It barely takes us an hour before my driver pulls into The Underworld parking garage that is our destination. He parks and waits, as he's trained to do. I own the building. The security here is above reproach, but I prefer it to be understated. Cameras and tech instead of burly guards reminding a person that they constantly had to watch their words, their actions, their tells.

Better for my purposes that they forget themselves.

I climb out of the car and take a step back, waiting for her to follow me.

I should know better by now.

Jasmine crosses her arms over her chest and glares. "Oh, I'm sorry. Was I supposed to heel?"

"A good pet would."

Her dark eyes flash in anger, and fuck if I don't enjoy it. She's beautiful in a fierce way that demands the attention of any room she enters—long wavy black hair, light brown skin, and a mouth made to wrap around my cock. Those lips form words that have my blood heating in response. "Fuck. You."

"I. Did." I bend down and snag her ankle, towing her across the seat. She tries to kick me in the face, her first show

23

of spirit since I put my shirt on her. It soothes something in me that I refuse to examine too closely. She's no good to me damaged. No matter what narrative she uses to attempt to write what happened, we both know the truth.

I pull her out of the car, spin her around, and bend her over the trunk. "Jasmine," I say mildly. "Tell me your safe word."

The slightest of hesitations, as if she wants to refuse me this. Finally, she spits it out. "Rajah."

I lean over her, letting the weight of my body pin her in place. "You wanted me to save you from the deal your father made. I did. This is my price." I could take her here, like this, and she'll curse me to hell and back, but she'll thrust back on my cock and scream my name as she comes.

It's not the time for that. I'm dancing on the edge of reason with her already, and any more tonight is a mistake. It takes several precious moments to reclaim control of myself. "We can stay here all night and fight if you want, but there's a meal, a bath, and a bed upstairs. The only person your resistance hurts is yourself."

"You're crazy if you think I'll sleep in your bed."

I chuckle, knowing it will make her see red. "A place in my bed isn't punishment, Jasmine. It's a reward. A reward you haven't earned. Not by half."

Her indignant huff makes me smile, though I smooth out my expression before I take a step back and allow her to turn around. She shoves her hair out of her eyes just so she can shoot me a glare. "You're a dick."

"And you're a brat." I motion to the elevators. "Want to continue to trade insults or do you want to go up?"

I can actually see her weighing her options before she turns and marches toward the door, every inch of her as regal as a queen. It's only then that I realize she's walking in this fucking place with bare feet.

I scoop her up, ignoring her curses, and move quickly to the elevator. Once we're inside, I set her on her feet.

She tries to punch me in the throat.

I laugh as I catch her fist. I can't help it. The woman never ceases to fight when she should flee, or to mouth off when she should shut up. True to form, she gives a snarl worthy of any predator. "Touch me again and I'll rip your fucking throat out."

So it'll be like that, will it?

I use my hold on her hand to yank her against my chest and then I band an arm across her lower back. She fights me, but there's no winning. Not with our size difference. Not when I'm so much stronger.

I wait for that realization to wash over her, for her to go still. It takes her longer to stop fighting than most, and even then she glares up at me as if I'm a bug she'd like to squash.

"You have the ability to stop this. One little word, Jasmine, and the game ends. That's all it's ever taken with us."

She clamps her mouth shut, though her anger doesn't appear to abate.

"Now that we have that settled …" The elevator doors open and I walk her backwards into my penthouse. I wait for the doors to shut behind me, closing off the exit unless one has the key, and then I release her.

She takes several large steps back. Though I can tell she wants to rip another strip off me, her curiosity gets the better of her. Jasmine turns in a slow circle. I follow her gaze, seeing the place through her filter. Wide open space with luxurious furniture, the color scheme minimalist in its extreme. Black furniture. White walls and pale wooden floors. The windows stretch the entire length of the penthouse, going from room to room, offering a view of Carver City.

That's where she heads.

I follow, keeping a few steps back, not bothering to turn on the lights other than the lamp next to the elevator. She reaches up, but stops before she touches the glass. "It's so big."

It's really not. Carver City isn't even in the top twenty of the largest cities in the country, but Jasmine doesn't care about that shit. This is the widest world she's ever experienced.

I can use that.

I'm just bastard enough to do it.

"Let's discuss terms."

She turns to face me slowly, as if it's a challenge to drag herself away from the view. "I was under the impression that terms were set when you growled that I was yours and then threw me over your shoulder like a piece of meat."

Fair point, but not one I'll admit. "Come now, Jasmine. You know it's not as simple as that. Didn't your father teach you anything?" A low blow, but it's imperative that this plays out the way I need it to.

She doesn't flinch. Of course she doesn't. There's very little I can say to her that her hated father hasn't already driven into her head. I've seen the way he talks to his daughter, as if she's shit on the bottom of his shoe. Good only for bargaining away her womb and legacy to the highest bidder.

Well, not the highest bidder. If he had, we wouldn't be in this situation to begin with.

She props her hands on her generous hips. "You have terms? Fine. I'm listening."

"You will not leave this building without permission. The penthouse and the floor below it are yours, but nowhere else."

Her eyes flashed. "So I've traded one cage for another. Wonderful. Just what I always wanted."

I ignore that. "Tomorrow, we'll see about you earning some clothes."

"*Earn* some clothes." Her jaw drops, but she recovers quickly. Jasmine shakes her head. "No. I'm not playing these games with you." She presses her lips together and then goes in for the kill. "You're even worse than he is."

No need to clarify which *he* she means. There was only ever one in her life. "He sold you to a monster."

"I don't think you should be throwing stones about *monsters.* And you were only too happy to jump in and use that to your advantage. Two sides of the exact same coin." She glares. "I'm not interested in playing."

I should have better control, should be able to stem the rising tide of anger within me. I didn't expect her to be grateful—I'm not delusional—but this is bullshit. "If one monster is just as good as other, would you rather I deliver you to Ali? I doubt he'll care that you're damaged goods as long as his end goal is achieved. He may even thank me for breaking you in, considering the shit he's into. "

I see the slap coming and do nothing to stop the blow. She puts enough force in it to turn my head. "Shut. Up."

She goes for another strike, but I catch her wrist. "No safe words with him, Jasmine. No way out."

"You're putting me in a cage. Don't act like I'm better off here."

It stings, even as I tell myself there's no reason for it to. I'm hardly an altruistic man. I may have changed my plan when news of the merger came through, but I always intended to take everything from Balthazar. The man is as much a monster as Ali is and, more unforgivably, he's bad at business. There's no reason he shouldn't own double the territory in Carver City that he does currently, but he's been too focused with petty bullshit to realize his potential.

That's fine.

His loss is my gain.

I study her. She's fucking exhausted. We could stand here and yell at each other all night, but it won't accomplish a damn thing. Taking Jasmine in the hallway of her father's home was an impulse I should have been able to deny, but she's always played fast and loose with my control. I handled it up to this point because the end game was more important than wanting to sink my cock into that tight little pussy while she went for my throat.

Now I get to have my cake and eat it, and I'm not even a little bit sorry about how things have played out.

"We'll fight about it tomorrow."

"I don't want anything of yours. I sure as hell don't want your charity." Jasmine unbuttons my shirt with shaking hands. A shrug of her shoulders and it's on the floor, leaving her gloriously, defiantly naked. She lifts her chin and stares me down. "You want a kept pet. Let's not pretty it up with whatever you had planned to keep me docile."

"Docile?" I shake my head and move toward her slowly, enjoying the exact moment she realized she miscalculated. A flash of something that isn't quite fear. Another woman would take that moment to backtrack, to try another angle. Not Jasmine. She all but shoots fire out of her eyes, as if she believes if she put enough anger and will behind it, she'll burn me to a crisp.

I sift my fingers through her hair and twisted it around my hand until I force her head back. I lean down, careful not to touch her anywhere but her hair. "You're about as docile as a rabid tiger."

"Then you're the fool who trapped that tiger in your home."

I don't bother to argue. She's right. Every little piece of my life is carefully calculated. It always has been. A man does not rise as far or as fast as I have by letting his baser instincts rise to the fore.

And yet, I want her.

I wanted her the moment I laid eyes on her five years ago, when I was first brought into Balthazar's operation. Twenty years old and as bold and beautiful as the flower she's named after. I knew better than to touch her then, no matter how much I enjoyed our verbal sparring sessions, no matter how often I read the invitation in her eyes.

She's shaking, and I'm not fool enough to think it's from desire. She's exhausted and beneath that mountain of anger is fear.

I force myself to move back, to release her. She's here, and that's enough for now. Jasmine's shaky exhale just confirms it was the right choice to make. I head toward the hallway. "This way."

"I really, really hate you right now."

I ignore that and walk deeper into the penthouse. Several seconds later, the sound of her footsteps padding after me make me smile. Even when she's fighting me tooth and nail, there's a core of submissiveness there that draws me, a moth to flame. Being burned to death isn't on the agenda. I'm in control, and the sooner she learns that, the smoother this will go.

The spare bedroom is rarely used. I'm not in the habit of allowing people into my home, let alone inviting them to stay for any length of time. When I fuck, I do it at the club. It saves me the trouble of anyone getting the wrong idea.

It's as neutral as the rest of my home. Clean lines, stark colors. The order of it soothes me. I hold open the door and stand aside, watching her expression as she takes the space in.

A small line appears between her strong brows. "What do you have against color, Jafar?"

"It's messy."

She arches an eyebrow, apparently forgetting that she's naked in my home. "Messy," Jasmine repeats. "You think color is messy." She shakes her hand and moves forward to investigate.

From tigress to curious kitten. All she needed was something to explore. I file away that information for later and content myself with watching her move through the room. She runs her hand over the comforter, testing its softness, and walks to poke her head into the walk-in closet.

The bathroom is what gets her. I knew it would. Balthazar might have been an asshole of a father, but he indulged his daughter's material desires without limit. Whenever she wasn't in her usual haunts, she could be found down by the fountain in the middle of his hedge maze. The whole thing is rather overdone for my tastes, over a square mile of curving paths and little courtyards, but it fit Jasmine's fancy. Or maybe she simply needed to pretend she wasn't walled in and the maze was her way of doing it.

I'll ask her eventually.

Not today, though.

I wait for her to walk back into the room to speak. "I have business to take care of."

She waves that away as if it's not worth knowing. "You always do."

Now's the time to establish what this relationship will be. "When I get back, I want you naked and kneeling at the front door."

She stops short. "Excuse me?"

"You heard me. Naked and kneeling. That's an order."

"When are you going to be back?"

I almost smile, but muscle the response down deep. "I'll be back before dawn."

"Before dawn," she echoes, understanding washing over

her expression. "You want me to wait for you. For an unknown amount of time. Naked and kneeling."

I permit myself a tight smile. "Yes, Jasmine. That's exactly what I expect." I turn around and head for the elevators. The thrill of the push and pull with her, the fighting and resisting —It makes me so fucking hard, I can barely see straight. If I had my way, I wouldn't leave her alone to stew over everything that's happened tonight, but business has to come before pleasure.

Even if pleasure with Jasmine *is* business.

I step into the elevator and ride it down to the parking garage. Jeremiah, my second in command, meets me there. He looks a little worse for wear, his suit rumpled and his normally perfect dark hair askew. I note the blood spatter on his shirt. "It's done?"

Jeremiah nods. "We ran into a few complications, but nothing the boys and I couldn't handle."

"Good."

He glances behind me at the elevator. "You got your princess?"

"Among other things." I head for the car and he falls into step next to me. "We're ready for the next part of the process."

He makes a face. "Ali slipped the net we cast for him."

I pause. "Find him." I wasn't exaggerating when I called Ali a monster. He and I might have started in similar places— fighting our way up from nothing—but the few lines I refuse to cross are ones he tramples over with glee. He's a sadist and a sociopath, his penchant for violence is only surpassed by his pride.

Taking Jasmine and dismantling his power grab will piss him off, and Ali is most dangerous when he's furious. The man is a loose cannon and he'll try to take Jasmine back. To take her from *me*. She's a toy ripped away from him before he got it out of the packaging, and it will only add to his rage.

And if Ali can't reclaim her?

He'll kill her.

"Find him, Jeremiah. Find him right fucking now."

CHAPTER 4

JASMINE

fter twenty-five years in the same few square miles of land, Jafar's penthouse is a revelation. I barely wait for the elevators doors to whisk shut before I give into my impulse to snoop. Easier to focus on that tiny pleasure than to think too hard about all the ways my life has gone up in flames.

My home is mine no more. If I could forgive my father for selling me in marriage—and I can't—I still can't forgive all the years of neglect and threats whenever I stepped too far out of line. Threats to carve away at the tiny list of my freedoms.

Now here I am, my leg in a different kind of trap.

I bypass the main living space and wander down the hall on the opposite side of the penthouse from my room. On the second door, I hit pay dirt.

I stand in the doorway for a long time, studying Jafar's bedroom. I don't know what I expected, but it's just as stark and beautiful as the rest of the house. I would bet good money that he had someone else decorate it. To his specifications, of course, but some of the little details feel off.

Not the paintings, though.

They're gorgeous.

I move on silent feet to stand before them. A trio, each in a deep red that sets something racing in my chest. Or maybe it's the content of the paintings. Each is a close-up of a woman's body. The first, the curve of her back. The second, a hip. The third, her breasts. The artist's name is a tiny scrawl near the bottom of each. *Death*.

Interesting.

I force myself to abandon the paintings in favor of finding juicier information. His nightstand is a bust. It's basically a small bookshelf. I peruse the titles but give it up for a lost cause. Jafar has a thing for nonfiction war stories. Of course he does. He probably reads them and takes notes before he goes into battle with his current-day enemies.

The bathroom is twin to mine, though his tile is black, rather than white. I snort. "Playing to type as always." The walk-in closet is filled with expensive suits, all arranged in a grayscale line from black to pale gray. It's the same with the shirts.

I briefly consider going back to the kitchen and taking a knife to every single one of them, but doing that now may be overplaying my hand. Best to save the true rebellion for later, when he'll undoubtedly do something to deserve it.

"Trust Jafar not to have anything remotely interesting in his room." I shake my head and walk back into the hall. Two more doors, and absolutely no reason not to explore them. The first leads to a powder room, also missing anything worth snooping in. The second is his home office.

"Pay dirt," I whisper. This is the room I need, not his bedroom. I should have realized that from the first. I glance down the hall toward the front door. He wants me naked and kneeling, a good little pet who obeys his every whim.

Worst of all, part of me wants to give him exactly that.

My body still aches from what he did to me, what we did together. I can play pretend that I didn't want everything he gave and more, but it's not the truth. I could have said no. Truly said no. I didn't.

I didn't want to.

I still don't want to.

I smile slowly. What will he do when I flout his order? Throw me to the ground and fuck me breathless again? Spank me? Maybe he'll force me to my knees, unzip his pants, and pound into my mouth until tears spring from my eyes and I can only submit or choke. I shiver, my skin feeling too tight, too sensitive.

Wanting the man who overthrew my father is a mistake. I know that even as I drop into his chair, the leather cool against my naked skin. A tap against the keyboard has the screen flaring to life. I'm not even a little surprised to discover Jafar has his computer password locked, even though it sits in a penthouse that is presumably inaccessible to anyone except for him.

Him, and now me.

I idly tap in a password, the most often used one according to things I've read. I don't actually expect it to work, but I've been surprised before. *Password1234.* The computer thinks for half a second before spitting out an Incorrect Password notification.

A little light appears at the top of the screen. Green, and then red. "Naughty Jafar," I murmur. Computers are something I enjoy, one of the few freedoms I was able to sneak past my father. I'm skilled enough to bypass my father's firewalls to order the books and things I want without his knowledge, but I'm mostly self-taught when it comes to anything resembling hacking. As such, I recognize what this is. An extra layer of protection. When the incorrect password is inputted, it either snaps a picture of the person at the computer or perhaps a video.

The fact that the light hasn't gone away suggests a video.

I stare directly into the camera. Caught. "If you didn't want me to snoop, you should have locked the door." I lean forward. "Or perhaps you shouldn't have brought me here in the first place." Talking to a camera that may or may not be recording feels foolish, but I'm still angry and hot and all tangled up from the events of this night.

The thought of Jafar seeing this video and rushing home to punish me … I lean back in the chair and spread my legs. "It's going to be a real shame if you can't actually see this." I could scoot the chair back to give the camera a better view, but I'm not in the mood to be even that good. He dumped me here as if I'm a sure thing.

I *am* a sure thing, and that only makes me angrier.

The phone at the desk rings and I jump. A quick glance at the computer tells me it's still recording. I use my free hand to pick up. "Yes?"

"That's not the proper way to answer a phone, Jasmine."

Oh yes, he knows I tried to get into his computer. "Mmm. Sorry, I'm a little distracted." I put some sugary sweet contriteness into my tone. "I'll be sure to take that criticism into account the next time I'm playing secretary."

Silent for a beat, as if I've surprised him. Surely he must know by now that even furious and scraping rock bottom, I can't help but come back swinging. No matter how unlikely my chances of victory.

"You're not following instructions."

I let the warning in his tone roll over me. Had I thought I was turned on before? It's nothing compared to now, to having him on the phone and knowing he can't touch me. I idly slide my finger through my wetness and up to circle my clit. "You're not back yet, Jafar."

A pause. There are men's voices in the background, but I can't quite make out the words. The noise dims as if he's moved into another room. "Tell me what I'll see when I review the recording."

So he *can't* see me right now.

Oh, this is just too delicious.

I use my foot against the desk to scoot the chair back farther. This should give him quite the show. "I'm sitting in your chair."

"Mmhmm."

"Naked." I barely sound like myself. What am I doing, playing this game with him? I should be fighting him every step of the way, should be demanding answers about what he's done with my father, and what he intends for the future.

Instead, I'm sitting here at his desk, fingering myself like the dirty little slut I can't help but be.

I slip two more fingers into my pussy, and I exhale harshly. "I'm fucking myself with my fingers."

Now it's his turn to exhale. "Naughty girl, aren't you? You're going to ruin my leather chair when you come all over it."

"Most likely." I bite my bottom lip to keep a moan inside.

"You know what happens to naughty girls?" He barely waits a beat. "They get punished."

My orgasm spirals closer. How many times have I laid in bed and touched myself just like this, imagining it's *his* blunt fingers shoving into me, spreading my pussy in preparation for his cock? Too many to count.

Having him on the phone, his voice growling in my ear?

It makes everything ten thousand times hotter. I let my head fall back against the seat, barely able to keep the phone to my ear. "I'm going to finger myself in here every time you leave me with idiotic orders like that last one." I slide my fingers up to pinch my clit and can't keep a gasp inside. "Maybe I'll do it on your bed next."

"Jasmine." His voice snaps like a whip. "Stop."

My hand lifts without my having any intention of obeying. I grit my teeth. "No." I force myself to ignore the command, to stroke my clit once, twice, a third time, until I'm coming with a moan I can't keep inside. It feels even better because he told me not to and I did it anyway.

I never have been good at following orders.

"Oops," I whisper.

Silence for several beats. When he speaks again, his voice is downright icy. "Remember, brat—naked and kneeling."

"Fuck off." I hang up, fear and need all twisted up in my head and heart and pussy. The light on the computer screen blips off, which is just as well, and exhaustion rolls over me. Too many things happened in the last few hours, too many changes. It saps my strength and leaves me confused.

I shouldn't want Jafar.

I know that. Of course I know that.

He's the snake tempting me out of Eden, except he barely has to crook his finger and I trip over my own feet in my eagerness to prove what a treacherous daughter I am. My father doesn't deserve my loyalty, but other people won't see it that way. Not after I've spent twenty-five years playing the dutiful daughter. And for what? So he can bargain me away to that bastard Ali?

Oh, Ali looks good, as long as no one examines beneath the surface. Handsome and possessing a smile that has charmed countless women out of their panties. He's also a liar and a thief and, most unforgivable of all, self-righteous enough to think he's better than the rest of us who move through the shadows.

To him, I'm a possession, a mark of his meteoric rise in this world. Balthazar's daughter, a jewel meant for a position in a crown. He doesn't see me as a person, and likely never will.

It's all over now. Jafar made sure of that.

Didn't he?

Surely Ali will bow out now, knowing this is a fight he can't win. He missed his chance with me, and moving on to easier pickings is the only thing that makes sense.

I wish I believe that.

I leave Jafar's office. There's nothing for me to find here, not until I know him well enough to figure out his password. Even then, I have no plan. Find information and blackmail him into releasing my trust fund? I have nowhere to go. No desperately needed knowledge of simply day-to-day things. I'm not even one hundred percent sure how to access the money even if the trust is still mine. How to get a job. How to use public transportation. I've never even been to a grocery store to shop for my own food. So many life experiences, and all beyond reach.

All *still* beyond reach.

The front door looms in front of me. It would be the easiest thing in the world to obey. It will feel good. I know that down to my very soul. It's different than my obedience to my father. That was given under duress, and I had no choice in the matter. This ... Jafar gave me a choice. It was a shitty choice, but a choice nonetheless.

I gambled.

I'm still not sure if I lost or won.

I close my eyes and imagine it. The cold marble against my already-bruised knees. The air conditioning drawing goosebumps along my skin as adrenaline fades and takes its heat with it. Of the door opening and Jafar walking through. Of ...

I'm not sure what comes next.

Will he fuck me right there on the floor again?

I shiver, and I can't pretend it's from anything but undiluted lust. Good girls aren't supposed to want down and dirty fucking like that. They aren't supposed to want to play on the dark side of desire, to push back until their partner forces submission, to love every second of the struggle.

I suppose I never was that good when it comes down to it.

Maybe that's why I turn on my heel and walk down the hall to my new room. Jafar wants obedience? He'll have to earn it. A single bargain does not a lifetime of servitude make.

It's all excuses. I smile and shut my door, taking the time to flip the lock. Jafar won't let this defiance stand, and he will more assuredly punish me, just like he threatened over the phone.

I can't wait.

* * *

THE SOUND of the door being slammed open jerks me into awareness. I never meant to fall asleep. Waiting for Jafar with a quip and a mocking smile is much preferable to this. I shove my hair out of my face and start to sit up, but he's already there, bracketing my throat and forcing me back down.

"I gave you an order, Jasmine."

He's not hurting me. Not yet.

I push against his hold, my heartbeat picking up at the pressure of his rough palm against my neck, of knowing how easily he could crush me. "I didn't feel like kneeling."

"Why am I not surprised?" He doesn't sound angry or out of control. No, he sounds just as coolly mocking as ever. It's disconcerting when compared to the rough way he rips the covers from my body. Even pinned down as I am, I can feel

his gaze rake over my nakedness. How can a man make m so hot from a single look? It defies explanation.

He trails a single finger down my chest between my breasts and stops just short of my belly button. "You aren't in control, Jasmine. You want me to come here in a rage and take it out on that tight little pussy of yours while you scream that you hate me and yet pull me closer all the while."

Yes, that's exactly what I want.

I press harder against his hand, needing the roughness, needing him to *touch* me. "It's not like I can stop you."

"No." For a moment I think he's agreeing with me, but he releases me instead. "That's not how this works."

I scramble up against the headboard, lust giving way to shame and embarrassment. He doesn't want me? The wild seesaw of emotions hasn't slowed down once since he walked into my room earlier this evening—or is it technically last night now?—and it doesn't show any evidence of doing so anytime soon. "What game are you playing?"

"One that requires clear rules." He gives me a contemplative look. "You're just a baby, Jasmine. You think you can throw a fit and flout the rules and still get what you want, to pretend I'm forcing you." Jafar shakes his head slowly. "Fuck that."

"Excuse me?"

"That play may have worked with your father, but it won't work now."

Frustration overrides my caution. "What is it you want from me, Jafar? Is it to have Balthazar's daughter waiting on you hand and foot? Is it to fuck me whenever you please and know each time I come for you that you've beat him?"

His slow smile does nothing to comfort me, but I doubt it's meant to. Jafar is hardly the comforting type. "What do I want from you?" He leans down until we're eye level. "Everything."

Everything.

"No," I whisper. I have so little that's mine and mine alone. I won't share it. I refuse to. How dare he ask me to crack myself open for his pleasure? Sex is one thing, even unconventional sex. This is something more and I want no part of it.

He glances at his watch as if he has somewhere to be. "Sleep for now. This afternoon, I'll have clothes brought in. Tonight, we're going out."

Under different circumstances, the possibility of going *out* might leave me breathless. Not now. Not like this. "I don't feel like going out."

"It wasn't a request." He turns and walks toward my door, which is when I notice it hangs at an angle from its hinges. It won't shut now, even if I try to force it. How he could display such violence and then switch gears to be calm and collected?

But then, Jafar has always had better self-control than I have.

He kicked down my door to prove a point. The same point he made by refusing to fuck me in punishment. Disobedience will not be tolerated or rewarded.

He pauses in the doorway. "Fight me if you need to, but I require nothing less than honesty."

"I *honestly* don't want you."

"Liar." He says it without heat. "We can keep playing the non-consent game if you like—*after* you earn it."

I climb off the bed. I can't have this conversation while I cower and he stands tall. Even across the room he towers over me, and I hate the thrill it sends through me. I point a shaking finger at him. "I'm not a dog you can reward with treats when I do a trick you like."

"No." He doesn't move, doesn't look away as I stalk toward him. If it wasn't for the heat in those dark eyes, I'd

think him completely unaffected. "Not a dog. A spoiled brat of a baby girl. Someone needs to bring you to heel, and I'll take great pleasure in doing exactly that."

Bring me to heel.

Red washes over my vision and I clench my hands into fists. Hitting him right now might feel very, very good, but one glance tells me that he'll never allow the blow to fall. I drag my hands through my hair and curse. "I hate you."

"No, you don't. You hate being trapped. It's hardly the same thing."

He has a point, but I'm not about to admit it. I prop my hands on my hips. "I have an easy solution. Give me my trust fund and release me, and we'll happily go our separate ways."

He shakes his head. "You agreed to the terms when you played our game. You lost, and now you're mine."

"You can't own a person!" No matter how hot the idea of being owned by Jafar makes me, I can't submit. I *can't*. He's upended my entire life. It may not have been the best life to begin with, but it was mine. Eventually I would have found a chance to fight my way out and leave all of it behind me.

To be free.

Something must show on my face because he slips his hand along the nape of my neck and tows me forward until we're nearly chest to chest. "Poor Jasmine," he murmurs. "Your dueling desires will tear you apart if you don't find a balance."

"Let me go."

He studies my expression. "Is that really what you want?"

Of course it is. Freedom is the only god I worship. "Yes."

"Prove it."

Understanding washes over me. He's reminding me of my safe word, of the full stop that comes when he pushes too hard and I need an exit hatch. I stare up at him, at war with myself. I want him. How could I not want Jafar? He's gorgeous and dangerous and forbidden in a way that tempts me all the more.

He's also put me in a cage the exact same way my father did. The only difference is the size and the rules that go with it.

In that moment, I truly do hate him. Just a little. "Rajah." The word is barely more than a whisper, but he instantly drops his hand and steps away, putting space between us that I'm still not sure I want.

It's too late, though. I've made my choice.

"Goodnight, Jasmine." He walks through the door without looking back.

Power and disappointment are strange bedfellows, but they are the twin emotions coursing through me. I knew he would stop, of course. But I can't figure out the tangle of emotions twisting through me, and suddenly I'm too tired to even try.

I stumble back to the bed and burrow under the covers. Tomorrow, everything will be clearer.

Tomorrow, I won't regret the choice I just made.

Most likely.

CHAPTER 5

JASMINE

*J*afar's gone when I wake. This time, there's no denying the disappointment. I'm a fool and a half for wanting him, for wanting to spend time with him, but I can't control my emotions. If that was possible, I'd be tempted to banish them completely.

I wander into the kitchen in search of coffee and find a pot waiting for me. The fridge contains my favorite creamer, newly purchased by the expiration date. I hadn't realized he noticed such small details. I don't think I've ever even seen Jafar in the morning before.

Not that it's morning now. I've slept past noon.

Next to the coffee maker is a sticky note with a schedule written on it in short, bold strokes.

2 P.M. - Stylist

8 P.M. - Be ready

Just that. Nothing more. Then again, I suppose I don't need to know more. As much as I want to bar the door against the stylist out of spite, the truth is that I need clothing. It's the only armor I've ever owned, and being without has me on edge.

I check the clock. I have enough time to shower and get ready to meet this stylist. Putting even that much effort exhausts me, but I can't afford to waver now. Not when I don't know what tonight—what the future—will bring. I need every weapon at my disposal.

An hour and a half later, I'm wrapped in a short robe nearly identical to the one Jafar ruined the night before, my hair done and my makeup impeccable. It doesn't escape my notice that Jafar had the bathroom stocked with my brands, all shiny and new.

He planned this.

I knew, of course. Jafar isn't one to leave anything to chance. But knowing that he ordered this room outfitted for me … I can't tell if I like it or loathe it. It seems to be an over-arching theme when it comes to me and Jafar.

The stylist shows up early.

She's a short, curvy woman with a pixie cut of blond hair and an attitude that conveys an instant chip in her shoulder. Her high-waisted trousers and fitted white blouse look classy and sexy at the same time, and she raises a single pierced eyebrow when she sees me. "Dear god, we have so much work to do."

"Excuse me?"

"No need to excuse anything, princess." She turns back to the elevator and snaps her fingers. Two hulking men wheel out rack after rack of clothing in a rainbow of colors. Another snap of her fingers and they disappear back into the elevator.

I can't tell if they're her men or Jafar's, but they obeyed her without blinking. I envy her that power. My father's men only ever obeyed me out of fear of him. I imagine Jafar's men will do the same. Never because of the threat *I* pose or the power *I* wield.

She arranges the racks in the living room and then points to a spot in the center. "Stand here. Robe off."

I don't move. I may bend to Jafar because I have no choice, but this woman is under the mistaken impression than I'm a cowering flower just waiting to be trampled. "Some courtesy would do you good."

The blonde rolls her green eyes. "Yeah, that isn't how this works. I'm the best at what I do, and being the best means *you* listen to me, not the other way around." She pointed to the spot again and injected enough sugar into her tone to give me a cavity. "Unless you'd rather walk around naked?"

She has me cornered and she knows it. I grit my teeth. I know better than to bargain from a weak position where I have nothing to gain and everything to lose. This is just a job to her. "If you don't dress me, you don't get paid."

"Cute." She smirks. "Contract says I get half up front. You throw a hissy fit, that money's still mine and I have a free afternoon. You don't have the leverage, so you might as well give it up now."

I hate that she's right.

I stalk to the spot she indicated and shrug out of the robe. The woman whistles. "No wonder Jafar lost his godforsaken mind over you." She circles me, his gaze calculating. "Jewel tones, yes. Look at that shade of brown skin. Perfect. Just perfect." As if I'm a piece of art, rather than a person.

I've botched this. I need allies, not enemies. I take a deep breath and do my best to banish my anger. It's not even directed at her, not really. She's just a convenient target that turned out to be not that convenient. "I'm Jasmine."

"I know." She rifles through the first rack. "I'm Tink. No, we can't be friends. No, I don't have any useful information for you to mine. No, I won't do anything to compromise my contract."

Well, so much for that offer of an olive branch. Strangely

enough, her abruptness has already started to grow on me. She's like being slapped in the face with an Arctic wind— cold and bitter and somehow refreshing all the same. "You have a contract with Jafar?"

She shoots me an exasperated look. "No, of course not. Who the hell has contracts with Jafar?" At my look of confusion, she frowns harder. "Holy crap, you really have no idea how this works, do you?"

"It might help if you explain," I say mildly.

Tink lifts up a red dress that seems more holes than fabric. She holds it up, nods to herself and sets it aside. "Not my job, princess."

"I'm not a princess."

"You're Jasmine Sarraf, daughter of Balthazar Sarraf. That's as close to royalty as it gets in Carver City. At least in Sarraf's piece of it."

It's not a point I'm willing to argue, because she's right. "How do you know Jafar?"

"Other than by reputation, I don't." She considers a green dress and puts it back onto the rack. Tink looks at me and sighs. "I'm not a comforter. We're not going to bond over our mutually shitty circumstances and become besties in the course of a few hours while I do the job I was hired to do. That's not how this works."

Silly to feel a sting over that realization. Sillier still to be so desperate for companionship that I reach out to anyone unconnected with my father who crosses my path. I sigh. "I won't put you in the difficult position of making small talk, then."

A ghost of a smile pulls at Tink's full lips. She really is a cute little thing, and full of the attitude of someone ten times her size. "You can small talk all you want. I just want to make it clear that I want no part of some harebrained escape scheme you're no doubt coming up with as we speak."

Curiosity sparks in me, a welcome relief to the confusion and anger. "Do your clients often come up with harebrained escape schemes?"

"My clients? No. Their women—and men, in some cases? Almost always." She shrugs. "The world is a strange place sometimes."

"Apparently." Oh yes, I'm curious now. I accept the red dress she hands me and pull it on. As Tink moves around me again, this time with pins and a concentrated expression, I can't help but ask my next question. "Have you ever been tempted to help?"

"Once," she answers around the pins in her mouth and then uses one to nip in the waist of the dress. "It didn't end well. Not for me, and not for them." She pins the other side and stands back. "Oh yeah, I'm good."

I look down my body. The red dress clings to me like a second skin, dipping down low between my breasts and even lower in the back. It's slit up both sides nearly to the hip. "It's indecent."

"Exactly." She frowns and adjusts the front of it, business-like despite the fact she has her hands all over my breasts. "You'll need tape for this." She frowns hard. "Then again, if you're going to The Underworld, tape is a shitty ass idea. Someone will end up ripping it off and then you'll have sore nips."

I blink. "I think you'll need to run that past me again."

Tink starts to laugh, but the sound dies almost immediately. Her green eyes go wide. "The Underworld. Carver City's worst kept secret, the sex dungeon to end all sex dungeons? The place where most of the business in this godsforsaken city goes down?"

I've never heard of such a thing. I know what sex dungeons are—I *do* read—but only in the most fictional sense. I had no idea that one existed in my city. Though, can it really be considered my city if I've never set foot in it? Jafar's penthouse might stand in what appears to be downtown, but it hardly counts as visiting. My father's home definitely doesn't count.

"Off with the dress." She gives an impatient motion with her fingers. Everything about Tink radiates impatience, but I suspect it's nothing personal. I should have recognized that from the beginning.

I carefully extract myself from the dress and pull on the next one she shoves into my hands. It's black and feels wicked against my skin. The V on this one isn't quite as deep, but it's short enough that I can't stop myself from tugging at the hem.

"Stop that." She smacks my hands. "You look uncomfortable and uncomfortable is not sexy. *Confidence* is sexy."

"I'm aware of that," I bite out. "Flashing my pussy at everyone I come into contact isn't my idea of a good time."

"You're missing out." She tugs the dress a little and nods to herself. "This one won't need adjusting. Good. You've got a rocking bod, princess."

That almost sounded like a compliment. "Thanks?"

"Nothing wrong with some of the stick-thin models I style. But nice to have a woman with actual flesh on her body for a change of pace."

I'm still not sure if she's complimenting me. I'm not sure it matters. I'll never be model thin. It's not something I ever aspired to. I've kept myself fit enough that my father wasn't making constant dark comments about my weight, but I like my curves. They aren't as generous as Tink's, but they exist.

Why do I care what this woman thinks of me and my body?

I push the thought away, already knowing I won't find the answer appealing. "Tell me about the Underworld."

"Not much to tell. It's your typical classy joint, except

people go there to fuck in kinky ways. Some of them are employed by the dungeon. Some of them are patrons."

"Is Jafar a patron?" I shake my head. "What am I saying? He must be if we're going there."

"Mmm."

Not an answer, but it turns out I don't need one.

At her motion, I exchange the black dress for a deep jade green one. And on it goes. Tink dodges most of my questions, but halfway through our time together, she actually stops insulting me. Progress, but I have the sinking feeling that I won't be seeing much of her in the future. How often does one need a stylist?

More accurately—how often does an owned woman need a stylist?

We finally settle on six dresses. They're all beautiful in their own way, and every single one of them would give my father a stroke if he saw them. The thought brings me a spiteful kind of pleasure, and I can't bring myself to feel guilty for it.

It's only as she's packing up that I realize what I'm missing. "We forgot underwear. And night clothes. And jeans." Something to wear in public.

"I didn't forget shit." For the first time since she walked through the door, she won't quite meet my gaze. "I brought what was ordered."

A kept pet has no need of underclothes or nightgowns or, apparently, street clothes. I pull my robe more firmly around my body and sink onto the couch. "I really am a caged bird, aren't I?" At least in my father's house, I could walk the grounds, could feel the open sky overhead, could pretend that the walls weren't really holding me captive.

I have no such option in Jafar's penthouse.

Tink hesitates and then moves closer. She looks up at me. "Look, you seem like you're not completely the worst."

"Thank you?"

"You're welcome," she says it without the least bit of sarcasm. "If you really want out of this thing with Jafar, you can make a deal with Hades. I can't say I recommend it, so you'd have to be hella desperate to go that route, but it's an option."

I swear, half the time this woman sounds like she's speaking nonsense. "Make a deal with Hades."

"He rules The Underworld. And yes, rules is the right word. He's a wily bastard, so don't let him catch you flat-footed." Something there in her expression makes me think that she was caught flat-footed, that she made a deal with this Hades.

How badly do I want to be out from Jafar's control?

Even if Hades was able to give me my freedom, I'll still be in the same predicament I would have if I took Jafar's deal. Freedom, but with no path forward. No money, no home, no *skills*. "Thank you."

"Don't thank me. I shouldn't have said anything." She shakes her head and finishing lining up her racks by the elevator. "Remember, princess. Confidence."

Something I had in spades in my father's home. At least when it came to dealing with other people. Never him. *A confident daughter is one who needs to be reminded of her place.*

I hate that his voice rattles around in my head despite my best efforts. He might have clothed and fed me, might have ensured I wanted for nothing, but he kept me from everything that mattered. Human companionship. Friends. Love. It might have been enough if he allowed me a real role in the business, but I was kept even from that. I'm his only child, and I *should* have been his heir.

I would have been if I was a son.

As a result of how tightly he kept me locked down, I'm as

awkward as a child trying to learn to walk. I should be better than this. I *can* be better than this. "Tink?"

"Mmm?"

"Would you—" *Confident, Jasmine.* "I'm going to need your services again. In a couple days. We'll have lunch and talk about the designs I'm thinking of."

She tilts her head to the side and studies me. "I'm expensive. You can't afford me."

"Let me worry about that."

She shrugs. "Then it's a deal. I'll be back at noon on Monday or Tuesday." She pulls a card out of her purse and passes it to me. It only has her first name and a phone number. "Call me after you've talked to him."

My face flames at the reminder that I have nothing without Jafar's permission, but I fully intend to extract a promise from him to allow this. It's the least he can do after everything I've given up.

Everything you wanted to give up.

I ignore the voice. "Thank you."

"Don't thank me." Again, she hesitates. "Wear the long red one tonight. It'll cause a riot."

I manage a smile. "I will."

The elevator doors open and the same men emerge to wheel her racks away. She doesn't look at me as the doors close, whisking her away.

I'm alone again.

After my entire life spent like this, I should be used to it. I had nannies and then tutors when I was a child, but all that stopped when I hit eighteen and gained my diploma. A woman only needs to know so much in order to play the role of wife, and that's all my father ever intended for me. He never wanted to hear about my ideas of bringing our business into the future, to utilize technology for our benefit. He never wanted to hear a single word out of my mouth except, "Yes, Father."

I take the dresses into my room and hang them up. They look absolutely absurd in the giant closet. A handful of bright colors against so much empty space. A quick check of the clock tells me that I have hours yet.

I could stay here and feel sorry for myself, or I could go explore the boundaries of my cage. Jafar said I have access to the top two floors, but he also said he owns the whole building. I'm sure someone will stop me if I try to move outside my confines, but I have to try. If only to see exactly where the perimeter of my limited freedom stands.

None of the dresses are suited for casual wear, but my only other option is the robe, which doesn't cover nearly enough of me. Yes, Jafar and I will be exchanging words once he comes back to the penthouse tonight.

I finally dress in the least revealing of the bunch, which really isn't saying anything. It's a deep purple dress that clasps around my neck like a collar and hugs every inch of me in the front, leaving absolutely nothing to the imagination. It dips low in the back and, like the red number, it has slits all the way up almost to the top of my hips. Sexy? Yes. Appropriate? Not in the least.

I step into the elevator and press the button for the bottom floor.

Nothing happens.

Second floor.

Same response.

I narrow my eyes. *That son of a bitch.* I start punching numbers, but nothing happens until I get to the nineteenth floor—the one directly below the penthouse. "I'm going to kill him."

The nineteenth floor is a smorgasbord of things designed to entertain. I find a small theater room with comfy reclining seats and a selection of movies large enough to keep me occupied for years. There's a small bar with a vast array of alcohols. A gym. A library. And a pool.

What it's noticeably lacking is *people*.

"A cage, indeed." A feeling in my chest, a fluttering like a bird that's had its wings clipped. Trapped. I am trapped. I may have been able to ignore the truth for the last eighteen hours or so, but I can't do it any longer.

I am worse off with Jafar than I was with my father.

CHAPTER 6

JAFAR

"*E*xplain to me again how you lost Ali for the *second* time."

Seth winces and looks like he wants to be anywhere but standing in front of me, delivering this particular bit of bad news. "We underestimated him. After he escaped the coup, we tracked him to his apartment. But when we broke in to collect him, he slipped away."

Fuck.

Fuck.

I keep my expression cold, letting none of the frustration through. Seth might have fucked this up, but he's still one of my best men. "Find him." The longer Ali remains free— remains alive—the greater the risk to Jasmine. If he was going to blow out of town, he would have done it by now.

No, he's looking to reverse the coup.

And he needs Jasmine to do it.

"Yes, sir." He ducks his head. For such a big man, he manages to occupy a small space in this moment. "I already have my men searching him out. He won't be able to evade us for long."

"Don't fail me." I wait for him to bob a nod. "Go."

"Yes, sir." He hurries from the room, leaving only Jeremiah.

My second shakes his head. "This isn't ideal."

"I know." I wait for him to point out that if we'd kept with the original timeline, none of this would be an issue. Five years of working my way close to Balthazar, close enough to strike, close enough to actually accomplish what I set out to when I came to Carver City, and I let my fury get the best of me when it mattered most.

Jeremiah doesn't say anything.

Of course he doesn't. He knows there's nothing he can say that I haven't already said to myself. I endangered my ambition because the thought of Ali getting his hands on Jasmine—of what he might do to her—made me lose my fucking mind. She's *mine*. She's been mine since I laid eyes on her.

I wouldn't do anything different.

"Find him, Jeremiah. I want you on this separately from Seth. He botched the grab the first two times. If he does it a third time, I don't want you to worry about extraction. Put a fucking bullet between his eyes."

"I'm on it."

There's nothing more I can do for the time being. At least on Balthazar's side of things, I have everything locked down. Most of his men were only too happy to jump sides. He made the cardinal mistake of not taking care of his own people, of looking to his wealth first and theirs not at all. It's why I chose him when I came to Carver City. There are other players that move just out of sight of the everyday world, some of them with more territory and more power than Balthazar, but he was the only one prime for the picking.

The fact that I laid eyes on his daughter and wanted her for mine barely came into the decision.

I check my watch. Jasmine's appointment with Tink should be long since wrapped up. The blonde is a pain in the ass, but she's the best in the business and discrete enough when it comes right down to it. She might go toe to toe with every single person she comes across, but she doesn't talk about clients with other people.

I have no intention of keeping Jasmine a secret. What's the point of possessing a rare desert flower if no one knows it exists? After tonight, no one worth mentioning will doubt that she's a prize worthy of burning cities to the ground over —or that she's already been claimed.

It doesn't take long to make it back to my building. I prefer to keep my operations as close as possible to the center of Balthazar's territory to stay on top of things. My territory now. It's important to keep one's thumb on the pulse of a place, and the only way to do that is to be neck deep in it. If Balthazar would have done that instead of living off in his mansion, he might have given me more of a challenge.

Possibly.

One of my men, Luke, meets me in the parking garage. "She's in the pool."

I nod my acknowledgement and head up. By now, she should be getting ready for our night, and her continued rebellion, though small, has my entire body going tight in anticipation. Jasmine is nothing if not a challenge, and that won't change anytime soon. The problem is striking the right balance of challenge and obedience. *That*, we haven't accomplished yet. That will take time.

Time we don't have.

Not with Ali circling.

The man should have been the least of my opponents. He's new enough to be shiny, all brash smiles and bold statements he has no way of backing up. It *should* have been simple to remove him and clear the path forward. And yet he's the most dangerous enemy I have currently. If Ali won't take the defeat lying down ...

Jeremiah will deal with it.

Should he fail—something he's never done to date—then I'll handle it personally.

I head into the pool area and stop just inside the door. The pool is meant more for recreation than for exercise, but Jasmine cuts through the water with the determination of an Olympic swimmer. I lean against the wall, enjoying this quiet moment of just watching. Jasmine and I have interacted countless times over the last five years, but they were always barbed comments that felt like a particular kind of inside joke. I was never able to just ... be in her presence. There was always someone watching, always some enemy skirting too close to the truth.

In most cases, the enemy was *me*, but that changes nothing.

I want this new normal. She's going to fight me until the day we die, but tonight will shift things into my favor. Jasmine fights because that's all she knows how to do—dig in her heels and make moving her more trouble than it's worth. I need to demonstrate the benefits of bending to my will. I relish the fight, yes, but she *has* to bend.

She finally registers that she's no longer alone and stops, treading water. "Jafar."

"Jasmine." I relish the wariness in her eyes. She's always looked at me like that, as if she sees beneath the carefully cultivated exterior to the man beneath. As if she knows exactly how dangerous I am, but she's not going to let that stop her from going a round or two with me. That look is what drew me to her in the first place. Beautiful women exist all over the world, but one who truly *sees* me? Priceless.

I slip my hands into my pockets. "It would be a shame if

we're late."

She shivers, obviously registering the threat beneath the mild words. "Do you honestly expect me to walk around naked when I'm not wearing one of those dresses?"

"I happen to prefer you naked."

Her dark eyes flash. "Is that so? I'm sure your men prefer the same." She swims to the shallow end, never breaking eye contact, and walks up the steps toward me.

Fuck, but she looks like a siren sent solely to torment me. As she rises out of the water, it cascades down her light brown skin, tracing a path I fully intend to follow with my mouth. In time. Her brown nipples are peaked and goose-bumps rise over her skin as the water reaches her hips, her thighs, and finally she's standing before me, defiant to the very end.

"My men know better." Despite my best efforts, my voice deepens, giving away *my* reaction.

Jasmine wrings out her hair and flips it over her shoulder. "Maybe at first. But normalcy breeds complacency. Eventually, they'll start looking. They won't be able to help themselves." She reaches up and tugs on my tie, straightening it. "Eventually they'll be tempted to touch."

She's baiting me.

Even knowing that, possessive feelings rise to the fore. "It'll be their life in payment for that touch."

"So dramatic." She tsks and moves away, giving me view of her generous ass. An ass that could send a man to his knees in order to worship it properly. I shake my head, pushing away my desire. Attempting to. Jasmine scoops up a white towel and starts drying her hair. "There's an easy solution, Jafar. Give me clothes. Then you don't have to worry about your men staring at my pussy every time I bend over." She gives me an innocent look, all large eyes and pouting lips. "I bend over a lot. It's distracting them."

"Show me."

She blinks. "Excuse me?"

"You bend over a lot, Jasmine? Seems to me that you like tormenting men simply trying to do their job." I force myself still, force myself to wait to see what she'll do.

Jasmine drops the towel. "Oops." She turns and bends at the waist to pick it up, moving slow, her legs parted just enough that, yes, I get an excellent view of her pussy.

"Don't move."

She freezes, her hand on the towel. "If I had clothes, this wouldn't be a problem."

I push off the wall and move toward her slowly. "If you think that, you don't know much about men at all."

"Well, I was a virgin until like twenty-four hours ago, so …"

Something like guilt rises in the wake of her words. Virginity might be nothing but a social construct, but her inexperience combined with my fucking her on the floor like we're animals? I press a hand to the small of her back. "Are you sore?"

She draws in a sharp breath like she's about to rip me a new one, and then curses softly. "I'm fine. Your cock is impressive, but not that impressive."

I smile, knowing she can't see the reaction. "Spread your legs wider. If you're going to give me a show, do it properly."

"You're so freaking bossy, Jafar. I should start calling you Daddy."

My cock goes so hard, I have to pause to keep from freeing it and driving into her right here and now. "You should." I palm her pussy, laughing hoarsely to find her drenched. Of course she is. Jasmine loves these games as much as I do, even if she fights me every step of the way.

Because she fights me every step of the way.

I scoop her up, ignoring her protests, and stride to the

elevator. A few minutes later, I haul her into her bathroom. "Stay."

"Bossy," she mutters.

I turn on the water, test the temperature, and then strip. Even with the time constraints in mind, I slow down, enjoying the way Jasmine's eyes go wide with every piece of clothing I take off. When I'm finally naked, I bracket her wrist and pull her into the shower. There's a tiled bench along one side of it, and that's my goal. I guide her down and crouch between her spread thighs. "Did you like Tink?"

She blinks. "Is that a trick question?"

I run my hands from her ankles up to her bruised knees and touch them gently. A quick kiss to each of them has her shaking in response. "It's a question requiring an answer."

Jasmine licks her bottom lip and allows me to arrange her on the very edge of the bench. "Tink is like one of those tiny, vicious dogs. She's short, but she might be the meanest person I've ever met."

"Mmm." I squeeze her thighs, urging them wider. "And did you like her?"

"Yes … Daddy." She says the word as if trying it out. Jasmine makes a face. "Why is that so sexy?"

"That's an answer you have to figure out for yourself." I mold my hands against her hips and up her waist to her full breasts. By now, she's shaking with need. I'd like an entire night to acquaint myself with her body, her reactions, *her*.

We don't have a night.

We have less than an hour.

I run my hands over her arms, noting the bruises on her elbows. I smooth a hand down the center of her body, between her breasts, over her stomach, parting my fingers to drag along either side of her pussy. "Are you going to be good tonight?"

She holds herself perfectly still, barely seeming to

breathe. "I don't know. I kind of enjoy being bad."

"I'm aware." I part her and idly run my thumb over her clit. "Nothing wrong with enjoying the fight, but the importance of obedience cannot be overstated." I finally meet her gaze. "You think you can control things by pushing and snapping and drawing the reaction you want. You can't. You want something? Ask for it. When I feel like you've earned it, it will be my pleasure to give it to you."

She wets her lips again. "Okay, fine. I'll play. Lick my pussy. Please."

Got you.

I dip down and give her a long lick up the center. Fuck, but she tastes divine. I should end it there, should prove my point, but I allow myself to suck her clit, to explore her with my mouth the same way I have with my hands. Her thighs quiver on either side of my head and fuck if I don't love how she's trying to be good and hold still, not wanting this to end any more than I do.

Unfortunately, we're on a time limit.

I give her pussy one last thorough kiss. Enough to pull her to the edge but nowhere near enough to push her over. Then I raise my head. "Be a good girl tonight and I'll reward you."

"You are such a bastard," she whispers.

I push to my feet and pull her up to join me. It's quick work to soap her up and then wash her hair. Another thing I'd enjoy taking more time with. Another thing I have to put to the side for tonight. For once, Jasmine doesn't fight me. She just stands there and passively follows orders. It won't last, but if I wanted a passive submissive, I could have found one long before now.

I shut the shower off. "Get dressed and meet me at the front door in forty-five minutes."

"Yes, Daddy." She uses the term as a weapon, sugary sweet

with a venomous center.

That's my girl.

I scoop up my clothes and stalk out of the room, leaving her staring after me. The temptation to turn around, to drag her to bed and play out a new kind of game, is almost too much to resist. I have to maintain control, though. Tonight is too important.

The Underworld is a sex club, but it's so much more complex than that. Sex is one of its main attractions, yes, but power eclipses all else. Every major player in Carver City has a membership there, and it's where we conduct deals over drinks and occasionally a blowjob. No violence is allowed, on threat of expulsion and being eighty-sixed for all time. All stand equal before the owner, Hades, and though the only territory *he* rules is The Underworld itself, he's arguably the most powerful person in the city.

Bringing Jasmine there sends a clear message to everyone who matters. Balthazar is out. I'm the new ruler of his territory. It also should cut Ali off from anyone looking to ally themselves with him.

It's more than that, though. I want to use our new standing to solidify power, yes, but I also want to see what Jasmine thinks of the club. Even watching her reactions as we drove through the city was a revelation. I can't wait to see the way her eyes go wide, to see what gets her hot, to explore with her.

I stop in the middle of pulling on a clean pair of pants.

Yes, I can enjoy myself tonight, but I can't afford to take my eyes from the prize. Getting lost in Jasmine, as appealing as it sounds, is not the endgame. In fact, it may just distract from the endgame.

I can't afford to be distracted.

Even by her.

Especially by her.

CHAPTER 7

JASMINE

*I*n between leaving me in my room to get ready and meeting me at the door, something changes with Jafar. He barely looks at me in my scandalous red dress before he whisks me down to the car and we're driving into the night.

I put it from my mind. A chance to be free of the penthouse is too important to worry about where his head has gone. It's not as if he'll confide in me. I'm a pet to be taken care of. Something occasionally entertaining, but nowhere near a full partner.

A full partner.

The thought seems ludicrous. Nowhere in the world I move in is there a chance for people to see me as anything but a possession. I *hate* that. Just because I have a vagina doesn't mean I wouldn't be as good a ruler as my father—better than my father. Instead, I am a pawn to be moved about on someone else's chessboard. My father ensured that before. Jafar ensures that now. He might as well slap a collar around my throat and attach a leash.

The thought sends a shiver through me. I wish with all

my heart I could say it's unpleasant, but the truth is far more complicated. I crave things I don't understand. Crave things I shouldn't.

Oh, I understand kink, at least in theory. I've read far and wide, and the books I invariable gravitate towards are hot enough to melt my e-reader. They spin fantasies that had me reaching into my drawer for a vibrator more times than I can count.

This is different. This isn't a story with a happily ever after waiting at the end.

Real life has no such guarantees.

Real life is messy and complicated and dangerous in ways that have nothing to do with my bodily health and everything to do with my soul.

"What's got you thinking so hard over there that you're not watching the city around us?"

I jump. I can't help it.

Jafar seems to melt out of the darkness on the other side of the town car. He's dressed to kill tonight, his black suit expensive and expertly tailored, his dove gray shirt beneath it pressed within an inch of its life. The clothing *should* dampen his dangerous aura, but somehow it only brings it into sharp focus. This man is a predator. No one with half a brain who looks at him will believe anything else.

He waits for me to answer, and I spend a useless moment waffling between truth and fiction. In the end, I know he'll accept nothing less than the former. "What is tonight supposed to accomplish?"

"I'm taking you to a sex club. It's going to accomplish you orgasming half a dozen times."

"Liar."

He arches his brows. "That's quite a tone you've taken." Mild. So mild as he issues his non-threats. If I keep pushing him, keep lashing out, will he punish me? Perhaps he'll put me over his knee right here in the back seat, shove my dress up and …

Focus, Jasmine.

I clear my throat, fighting for control. Fighting to appear just as calm and collected as he is despite the fact my heart wants to thunder right out of my chest. "You are perfectly capable of bringing me to orgasm half a dozen times in the penthouse. You have an agenda for tonight, and I would like to know what it is since I'm taking part in your plans."

He reaches out and idly twines one of my curls around his finger. "You saw Tink today. What did she tell you about The Underworld?"

I notice that he didn't question that she told me something. I wonder how well he knows Tink, and something hot and ugly flares to life beneath my skin. Jealousy. The realization almost makes me laugh out loud. As if I have any claim on this man.

No, he holds all the cards, all the claim, all the power.

Am I even allowed to protest if he fucks someone else?

The thought leaves me cold.

I swallow hard, trying to focus on the question he asked me. "She didn't say much. It's owned by someone called Hades. He makes deals?"

"Mmm." Jafar releases my hair and sits back, depriving me of even that minimal contact. "Hades is dangerous, Jasmine. You won't look at him and think it, but he's the biggest threat in The Underworld."

"Then why are we going?"

"Aside from the fact that it's the best dungeon in the state and I want to play with my mouthy little brat?" A flash of his teeth in the shifting shadows, gone almost as soon as they appeared. "Everyone who's worth killing is in that dungeon. There are rules that no one dares fuck with, but it's a good place to go and scope out the enemy. Tonight, it's about cementing my position."

Understanding dawns, leaving a sour taste on my tongue. "You want everyone to know you staged a coup of my father's territory." I lean back, needing more distance between us. "You're going to show me off, a war prize for your efforts."

"Yes."

I haven't forgotten the reality of this arrangement. Of how it came to be. I look out the window. "Did you kill him?"

"Why do you sound so wretched, Jasmine? He wasn't a good man. Fuck, he makes *me* look like a saint with some of the shit he did." He moves closer, touching my chin to bring my attention back to him. This close, I can almost see his expression clearly, but it gives nothing away. Nothing except the way his gaze bores into me as if trying to impart some vital information. "He hit you."

"You didn't answer my question."

"You would forgive me if I had murdered him?"

It's still not an answer, but I reach deep for the truth. There's a curious blankness when I think about my father. A veil I can't pierce and have no interest in trying. "If you didn't, you are leaving an enemy at your back."

A pause, the barest of hesitations like I've surprised him.

I smile, though there's no heart in it. Maybe there's no heart in me, either. "My father is a terrible person. You worked for him long enough to know the truth." He would have sold me. He *did* sell me, despite my protests. I can rail against Jafar until the end of time, but the truth is that I chose our deal, even if I didn't fully realize the parameters of it. My father didn't give me a choice. He would have handed me to Ali and never looked back as long as the contract went through.

One less thing for him to worry about.

I lean back in the seat. "He murdered my mother. Did you know that?"

"Yes."

Of course he did. It was one of the worst kept secrets in that huge house. The official story is that my mother died from a sudden sickness. No one's cared enough to question it. One day she was there, the next, she was gone, leaving a hole I'm not sure I'll ever fill. "Did you kill him, Jafar? Answer the question."

This time, he doesn't hesitate. "Yes. As you said, he was a threat. If he'd gone quietly, it might have played out a different way."

My breath leaves me in a whoosh and I can't quite manage to reclaim it. I press my hand to my chest, my head going light. "Oh."

He's there instantly, gripping the back of my neck and guiding my head down to my knees. "Slowly, Jasmine. Inhale. Yes, like that."

It takes several laborious inhales before I can speak again. "I should feel bad. Angry. Sad. Something." I give a slightly hysterical giggle. "I don't feel anything at all." My father was a monster. At his very best, he was neglectful and absent. His *best*. "You're right. I'm a horrible, traitorous daughter."

I barely hear Jafar's sigh and then he pulls me onto his lap. I resist at first, but he's stronger and the truth is I don't *want* to resist. I giggle again, the inappropriate sound horrifying me almost as much as my complete lack of grief over the situation. "A traitorous daughter and her father's murderer. Maybe we really do deserve each other."

"We do." The way he says it, as if it's fact and not words meant to comfort. But then, Jafar has proven himself to be shit at comforting.

That's okay. It's hardly in my skillset either. Who would I

comfort? I have no friends. No family. The only human contact I've had are my father's men and Jafar.

I shiver and he wraps his arms around me tighter. "I hate my life."

"Shh." His lips at my temple, the steady beat of his heart against my back, the strength of him forcing my body into stillness. "Tell me what you need."

"A friend." The silly request pops out before I can think better of it. I shake my head. "I really am pathetic."

"Not that, Jasmine. Never that."

Strangely, his attempt to comfort me only makes it worse. "I'm not free, Jafar. What am I supposed to do? Ask you to set up playdates?"

His lips curve against my temple. "It can be arranged. Play by the rules and I'll reward you."

I shift, belatedly realizing that his cock is hard against my ass. Heat rolls through me, and I welcome it with open arms. Easier to focus on sex than the reality that I can't escape.

That I'll never escape.

I roll my hips. "What are your rules?"

"They're simple enough. In fact, there's only one. Obey."

Obey.

His grip on me shifts, one hand falling to where the slit in my dress has bared my hip, the other cupping my breast through the silky fabric. "Tonight, you'll be silent and obedient." His fingers find my nipple and pinch, drawing a gasp from my lips. "Keep your head down, regardless of what you hear, and obey my commands."

"What do I get if I do?"

His chuckle makes my whole body go tight. Jafar slips his hand beneath my dress and palms my pussy. He pushes two fingers inside, possessing me completely. "I'll take care of this pretty pussy tonight."

I can't breathe. "And if I don't?"

Just like that, his hand is gone, leaving me empty and wanting. "Then you'll get a punishment." His voice goes dark, any hint of amusement drifting away like smoke. "You like to be punished, but I don't reward bad behavior. If you disobey, the punishment won't be one you'll enjoy."

Even though I know he's serious, his words still fan the flame of desire heating my blood. "How do you know what punishment I will or won't like?"

"You're going to tell me."

I blink. "What?"

"Choose your reward tonight."

That wasn't what I asked. My mind goes in a thousand different directions, scrambling over itself to provide the best answer. "I want …" I swallow hard and try again. "I want it like it was before. I want you to force me."

"Chase you." His thumb circles my nipple. "Pin you down and shove the dress up around your hips." He moves his other hand back to my pussy, but instead of fucking me with his fingers, he keeps his touch light. A single finger circling my clit the same way his thumb circles my nipple. Again and again, a tortuously slow circuit.

"Yes, Daddy," I gasp.

"Good girl." He sounds completely unaffected by what he's doing to me, and somehow that only makes it hotter. I can *feel* how much he wants me, but his voice and his touch are both so distant and casual that this whole situation becomes a thousand times dirtier.

As if I'm just a toy for him to play with.

I'm panting now. I can't seem to stop. "Please."

"Please?" He nips my earlobe. "Do better. You have more than enough words when you're pissed. Tell me what you want."

"Your mouth." What's supposed to be a demand comes out like a plea. It's as if a dam breaks and suddenly all I have are words. "Lick my pussy, Daddy. Please make me come."

"You want your reward before you earn it."

I strain my hips, but I can't get him where I need him. I'm so close, and yet so far from what I need. "I'll be good. I promise."

"Mmm. We'll see." He drops me on the seat and shoves me back against the door. "Lift your dress and spread your legs."

I scramble to obey, lust making it impossible to think about fighting him on this. He wrenches my legs wider yet and I have to reach overhead to the handle above the door to keep from sliding down the seat.

Jafar dips down and I can feel his breath against my clit. "Ask me again, baby girl."

Baby girl.

God, it feels downright wicked to play like this. Wicked and a little wrong, but so incredibly right. I gulp down a breath, trying to hold still. "Lick my pussy, Daddy. Please make me feel good."

He wedges his hands beneath my ass and lifts me to his mouth. The first swipe of his tongue leaves me weightless and giddy with relief. Back in the shower, Jafar was only playing with me. Teasing.

He's not teasing right now. He spreads me wide and tongues my clit as if he knows exactly the touch I need to get me to the edge. Pleasure rises in a wave I try to fight, try to resist. I don't want it over yet. I want this moment to last, to draw out this wickedness, to keep feeling dirty in the best way possible. Jafar is tonguing my pussy in the backseat of a town car because I called him Daddy and asked really nicely.

If this is his idea of a reward, maybe I should have been playing by his rules all along.

I can't hold out any longer. I come with a gasping cry. "Oh

god." He keeps tonguing me for several long moments, gentling his touch until it's the lightest of kisses.

Jafar sits back and pulls me to straddle his lap. When I go to grind down against his cock, he stops me. "You'll make a mess." His lips quirk. "You already have."

"Sorry, Daddy." The title falls easier from my lips. Naturally.

"No, you're not." He swipes a thumb across his bottom lip, where I can still see evidence of my orgasm there. He presses his thumb into my mouth, and I suck him eagerly. I've tasted myself in the past before. Of course I have. It was never this sexy before.

Before I can think better of it, I dip down and lick along his bottom lip. And then his top. Jafar holds perfectly still as I clean myself from his face, the only evidence of how affected he is in the bruising grip he keeps on my hips.

When I finally lean back, he gives a rasping chuckle that goes straight to my clit. "Fuck, baby girl, you better be good tonight, because I'm as eager for that reward as you are."

"I'll be good, Daddy. I promise." I want his cock. I want him to force me down and drive into me. I want so many things. Things I've barely allowed myself to fantasize about. It felt too cruel to do it before, to want something I was never going to be allowed to have.

With Jafar, I might just earn it.

He pulls a handkerchief out of his pocket and finishes cleaning his face, his beard. It's only then that I realize the car has stopped, has been still for quite some time. Jafar sets me aside and arranges my dress. "Remember. Eyes down. Obey."

"Okay," I whisper. An orgasm is a release, a little death. Coming hard enough to make my limbs loose and my head spin should take the edge off my desire, should draw me back to earth where I belong.

It doesn't.

I want him more now than I ever have. It's a sickness in my blood, making me woozy and almost drunk. "Jafar?"

He pauses, his hand on the door. "Yes?"

"How can this possibly work?"

He doesn't answer. Instead, he opens the door and steps out, leaving me with more questions than answers.

Leaving me with no answers at all.

CHAPTER 8

JASMINE

From the little I know of The Underworld, I half expect to climb out of the car and find myself in front of an old Victorian mansion. Something that hints at the inner goings on within its walls.

It's nothing of the sort.

I look up, craning my neck to take in the sleek building that climbs to touch the sky. It's almost as if this Hades takes his mythology more serious than most. He may rule The Underworld, but he's built his very own Mount Olympus. Tink's words from earlier come back to me. If I truly want out of this trap with Jafar, Hades may be my only option.

I close my eyes for the space of a breath, striving for clarity, striving to *think*. But Jafar presses his hand to the small of my back and any hope of rational thought flits away into the night. He guides me to the front door. I see no one, but it clicks unlocked the moment his hand touches it.

We enter a small lobby with a desk and two rows of elevators. It's all pale gray walls, darker gray marble floors, and stainless steel of the desk. Stark. A little cold. I shiver. "This whole place is The Underworld?"

"No."

The touch of his hand moves me to the left bank of elevators. We ride up to the thirtieth floor and step out. The color scheme is more of the same here. Gray walls, black floor, a white desk that holds one of the most beautiful men I've ever seen. He wears a white button-down shirt that sets off his dark skin and his black hair is cut close to his head. He looks up and his eyes warm at the sight of Jafar. "Welcome back. Is there anything particular you're looking for tonight?"

I remember myself at last moment and drop my gaze to the floor. Jafar's thumb rubs a small circle again my back, as if he sees and acknowledges that I'm obeying. Or perhaps I'm looking too far into things. His voice is certainly unaffected when he speaks to this man.

"A drink, a show. Maybe a room later."

"Perfect." I watch him type something into his tablet. "Enjoy your stay."

"I always do." Charm emanates from him, and the man smiles in a dazed sort of way that I sympathize with. Jafar doesn't bother to charm me. Or maybe he knows I have no interest in the smooth lie he can create with his voice and smile.

I've had more than enough lies to last me a lifetime.

We walk through the large black door and into another world.

Oh, it doesn't overtly look like another world at first. A circular bar surrounds a sculpture I can't quite wrap my mind around. Deep booths line both walls, bathed in shadows from the intimate lighting of the room. It seems rather mundane, until I finally get a good look at the sculpture and stop short.

It's an orgy.

I frown, trying to count limbs, to match them to people, but I give up at seven. I want to move closer, to see it in all its glorious detail, but Jafar makes a low noise before I take my first step. Right. Obedience. I am not allowed to wander about with wide eyes. It's not wise, even if there weren't his rules to consider. A lamb in the woods is as good as dead, and if this place is populated with people like Jafar, then that's exactly what I am.

Prey.

Jafar steers me toward the bar. There are other people around, but with my eyes down I only get the impression of suits and a few flashes of bold color in the dresses. No one is wearing red, and I feel like a drop of blood in a pool of sharks with the way attention shifts to me and narrows. It's not entirely unpleasant, but the feeling of so many eyes watching my every breath has me shivering.

"Sit."

I carefully perch on the chair next to the bar. Jafar remains standing and drapes his arm over the back of my chair. Casually possessive in a way that might irk me if we were alone, but that I appreciate in this room.

I crave experience. I want to throw myself into the world with delight and fury and grasp all the things denied to me up to this point. Why am I sitting here, shaking like a leaf before the summer storms? I close my eyes and try to breathe through it, but the fluttering feeling in my chest morphs into fear. True fear.

Jafar's hand closes around the back of my neck. Not harsh this time, but a grip tight enough to hold me in this moment. "Breathe, baby girl. They're just looking."

I shiver again. I can't help it. Even though it's wiser to stay silent, to cling to the few cards I have left, words spill from my lips. "I don't understand this."

"You were locked up a long time."

I open my eyes to glare. "I'm still locked up."

"Yes," he answers simply, without the least bit of shame.

"What can I get you?"

He glances at the bartender, a Hispanic woman with her hair in a high ponytail who wears what seems to be the uniform in this place—a white button-up and perfectly tailored slacks. "Scotch for me. Whiskey for her."

He knows my drink. How could he possibly know my drink? One of the many restrictions my father put on me was limiting my access to any kind of food or drink he deemed unhealthy. Alcohol and fried food topped the list. I couldn't get access to the kitchen without someone reporting on me, but over the years, I would pocket different bottles to try out. Whiskey became a personal favorite.

I look at him, searching for something I already know he won't give freely. Jafar remains an enigma to me, but I can't help grasping at these little details he drops. Proof that he wants me as more than a simple trophy of war.

Or perhaps I'm reaching because I crave companionship so desperately, I'm willing to bend over backwards to paint him in a flattering light.

The bartender deposits our drinks and moves around the corner. Jafar still has his hand on the back of my neck, but I don't have the strength to tell him to release me. Not when his touch is the only thing holding the panic at bay. I can feel it there, bleating in terror just out of reach.

"Drink." He watches me lift the glass with shaking hands and drain half of it. The whiskey burns my throat, but I welcome the fuzzy warmth it will bring. I go for another drink, but he touches the top of the glass, stopping the movement. It's a gentle touch. I could ignore his clear order and drink more.

I set the glass back on the bar. "I wasn't finished."

"When's the last time you ate?"

I blink. "I'm not sure. I was nervous about tonight."

He nods as if I've revealed more than I meant to. "I don't

want you shit-housed, Jasmine. That was enough to take the edge off."

"But—"

He pushes my glass out of reach. "You can have more later —after you eat something."

I narrow my eyes, but it's difficult to be furious with him when the whiskey has already fuzzed the edges. I'm not drunk. Nowhere near drunk. But I don't feel in danger of fleeing any more.

"Jafar."

His hand on my neck keeps me from turning, but he rotates me to face the woman behind us. I get a glimpse of purple and bare feet out of the corner of my eye, but nothing else. When he answers her, he's the coldly polite man I first met five years ago. "Megaera."

"Hades wants a look at your spoils of war." Amusement filters into her dry tone. "Pretty little thing, isn't she?"

"Pretty doesn't begin to cover it. She's exquisite."

They're talking about me as if I'm not here, or as if I have no more agency than the chair I'm perched on. I want to snap back, to snarl that I'm a person with my own thoughts on things and not a *pretty little thing*.

Except I promised to obey.

I take a slow, silent breath. I can do this.

"May I?"

Jafar rotates my chair to face the room and uses his hold on me to nudge me to stand. "By all means." He gives me a small squeeze and drops his hand, though he remains close enough that I imagine I can feel the heat coming from his body. A small anchor I cling to as I try not to shake.

A single soft finger presses against my chin, lifting my face. I look at her. I can't help it. They call me exquisite, but this woman is something else entirely. She wears a purple dress that's almost Grecian, but I suppose that's to be expected with the theme of this place and the man who rules it. She's all sharp features that aren't in the realm of traditionally pretty, but there's something about the way she holds herself that leaves flutters in my stomach. Lower.

Blue eyes study my face in pieces. Eyebrows, eyes, nose, lips. She strokes my chin almost absently and I can't stop my shiver. The woman—Meg—laughs. "You're right, Jafar. She's exquisite. Are you going to share?"

I can't move, held captive by her touch, her gaze. But I hear Jafar's amusement rise to match hers. "It appears my baby girl's not averse to the idea."

"Baby girl." Meg smiles, the expression just as sharp as the woman herself. "I look forward to playing with you when your Daddy gives permission."

Playing with you.

I can't stop shivering. I shouldn't want that, to be shared, should I? I have no idea. My fantasies are only in theory at this point, except for the ones Jafar and I have played out together. Have I touched myself to the thought of more than one pair of hands on my body? Yes. Oh, yes.

But the thought of doing it now? Tonight?

"That's enough."

Meg drops her hand and steps back. If anything, the interest in her eyes has increased from this little exchange. "Don't keep him waiting long." She turns. I can't help watching her walk away, can't quite seem to pull my gaze away.

"She has that effect on people."

I twist to look at Jafar, my emotions ranging from desire to disbelief. "You'll share me."

He shrugs a single shoulder. "It's open for negotiation."

"You told her that you'd share me."

"Come here." He waits for me to obey, to step between his thighs, to set his hands on my hips. "You want her."

"I—"

"The truth, baby girl."

I almost look back in the direction Meg walked before I catch myself. "She's beautiful."

"She's beautiful when she sucks cock, too." A small smile pulls at the edges of his lips. "And with a whip in her hands. Meg has many facets."

He speaks with a kind of knowledge that suggests they have some sort of history. He's had sex with her, has had his cock in her mouth. Jealousy spikes, joining the lust and confusion making me woozy. "You've fucked her."

Jafar studies me long enough that I have to fight the urge to squirm. "Yes, I've fucked her." He leans down until his lips brush my ear. "And now she wants to fuck you. Meg has a thing for ropes and denied orgasms. If I give her permission, she'd tie you up and lick that pretty pussy until you're begging her to let you come. And she won't do it. She'll take you to the edge over and over again, until your pleasure is just as sharp as any pain." His fingers skate down my hips to the top of the slits on either side of my dress, until he wraps a hand around each of my thighs. "I'll watch, and when you're at the breaking point, she'll untie you and you'll crawl to me. If you ask very, very nicely, I'll fuck you while Meg licks that sensitive little clit of yours. A reward for being a good girl."

"I…"

He dips his hands down farther, his thumbs dangerously close to my pussy. "You're wet, baby girl. Do you know why?"

Is there a correct answer to his question? I have no idea. "No?"

"Because you want what I just described. You think you shouldn't, but you do." He returns his hands to my hips and I can't stop the protesting sound that flutters in my throat. Jafar raises a single eyebrow. "Not tonight. I'm not in the mood to share you yet. But when I am?" Another of those shrugs that mean everything and nothing. "Maybe I'll let Meg have her fun. Or maybe I'll order you to suck Hook's dick while I fuck you. The options are endless, baby girl. Fucking *endless*." He pushes slowly to his feet. "Trust me to take care of you. It's as simple as that."

As simple as that.

I might laugh if I could find the breath to inhale. Every experience I've had with Jafar has proven time and time again that I can't trust him. Not true trust. Do I believe he'll hurt my body in a way I don't want? No. I crave his touch and I crave the power games we play out.

But trust him with my heart? My soul?

I'd have to be the biggest fool in the universe to hand those parts over to him. To hand *anything* to him that I don't absolutely have to. I have so little power in this world. If holding back means I maintain a little of it?

I can't afford to do anything else.

CHAPTER 9

JAFAR

I knew I'd have to go through this song and dance the first time I brought Jasmine to The Underworld. I *counted* on it. I can take or leave playing in public, so attending a dungeon isn't on my list of must haves solely for the sex. Having a membership so I can keep my thumb on the pulse of the city? That's worth the hefty fee I pay every month and any grandstanding Hades requires.

It doesn't stifle my irritation as I press my hand to Jasmine's back and guide her in the same direction Meg took a few moments ago.

My baby girl wants to be shared, and from her reaction to Meg, she's just as much a fan of women as she is of men.

I didn't anticipate that.

I turns out I didn't anticipate a lot of things when it comes to Jasmine Sarraf.

"Remember the rules," I murmur.

"I remember." On cue, she drops her gaze to the floor. I don't need that shit the same way some people in this place do, but I can't deny a thrill at the easy obedience. It's likely only because she's overwhelmed and probably over-sensitized. If the floor felt steady beneath Jasmine's feet, she'd already have swung at me, have pushed me until I was tempted to fuck her right there against the bar to prove a point. She loves dancing on my buttons, and I can't quite manage to hold it against her.

I push open the door and hold it while she walks through next to me. Hades does a round through the lounge once a night, but he mostly stays in his private lounge if he's in the mood to entertain. The nights he plays in the public rooms, though, are the kind of nights that draw a crowd. It takes a specific kind of person to hold this place together with the amount of power that moves through its doors, and Hades has the personality for it in spades.

His button pushing irritates the fuck out of me.

The lounge is decorated in the same expensive understated tone as the main room. Sturdy leather furniture, thick carpet, dim lighting except for the trio of sculptures lining the back wall. I hate the low lighting. It gives the feeling of not being able to see the truth, and I have to keep reminding myself not to squint and give even that much reaction. I prefer to see everything in startling clarity. Hades is a fucking romantic.

He waits for us in his favorite chair, a giant piece that could easily fit three people fucking. It has in the past. Tonight, he's got Meg kneeling at his feet, the very picture of a subservient submissive, her eyes downcast and her hands neatly folded in her lap. Hades sits forward as we cross the room, and I have to fight the urge to step in front of Jasmine to shield her from his gaze. He claims to know what his people want before even they do, to divine kinks as if by magic. The truth is he's simply excellent at reading people and body language. No magic required.

It doesn't stop him from dazzling newbies.

"You're right, Meg. She's exquisite." He turns that penetrating look in my direction. "It would take someone special to sideline our Jafar, though, so I suppose that's to be expected."

"Hades."

"Let your baby girl come closer, Jafar. I want a better look at her."

I bite back a sigh. I shouldn't be surprised that Meg basically sprinted back here to report on everything we spoke about. She's Hades's creature, through and through. It'd be a damn shame if she didn't seem so pleased by that fact most of the time.

"Go ahead," I pitch my voice low, though there's no way Hades won't hear. No doubt he can see the fine shakes working through Jasmine's body from where he sits. Desire, yes, but she's taking in so much, so fast. Too fast. Something else I should have anticipated. The woman has been locked up her entire life, and introducing her to the world outside her father's walls should be done in small sips, no matter how she chafes at the restraint.

Bringing her here is the equivalent of throwing her off the deep end and expecting her not to panic. At least she trusts me enough to find my touch anchoring, even if she doesn't realize that's what's happening.

If anyone realizes how precarious our balance is at this moment, it would be child's play to knock us both on our asses. I hold myself perfectly still, as if she is just another sub, I'm just another Dom allowing the master of this place to investigate my property.

"Come closer, child. I won't bite." Hades grins, his white teeth flashing against dusky skin. "At least not unless you ask very nicely."

Jasmine takes the last few steps that bring her nearly close enough for Hades to touch. He doesn't. He's too well-mannered for that under usual circumstances, though I can see the calculation in his dark eyes, already considering how to use this development to further his interests. "Jasmine." He says her name as if he can already taste her on his tongue.

I take a step forward before I catch myself. *Damn it.*

Hades grins at me. "Got you." He turns back to Jasmine. "Jafar has been a hard nut to crack. He fucks like a champ, but getting into that deliciously conniving brain of his? Impossible. And here you come, this near-innocent with a taste for ..." He inhales deeply as if taking in her scent. Her very soul. "Rough play. Very, very rough play. You like him to force your subservience." His voice deepens. "I approve."

"That's enough, Hades." It doesn't matter how he figured it out. I won't have him stripping her bare here, not while she and I are on such fragile ground.

Hades's grin turns knife-sharp. "Caged birds always crave the sky, Jafar. You'd do well to remember that." He takes Jasmine's hand and presses his lips to her knuckles. "You're always welcome here in The Underworld, Jasmine Sarraf. If you ever want to bargain, I'm more than happy to make time for you." He grins against her knuckles. "And if you want to play with our Meg, I'd be delighted to arrange that as well."

"Hades."

"Yes, yes, I'm overstepping. Can't let your prisoner know that there's a trap door within reach, can we?" He finally releases Jasmine's hand, but he coasts his thumb over her knuckles in a casual move that sends my blood pressure through the roof. There's no reason for it. Hades is casually intimate with everyone until he's not. His touching Jasmine means nothing. Her catching her breath at the feeling of his lips on her skin means jack shit.

I have absolutely no reason to be jealous.

That doesn't stop me from snapping my fingers at her. "Attend, baby girl." A reminder of whose hand holds her leash.

CHAPTER 10

JASMINE

*a*cross the room, the woman—the Domme—finishes the spanking and is stroking her hands along the tender flesh of her submissive's ass. She reaches between his thighs to cup his balls, and there's no mistaking his enthusiasm at her touch.

It's so much hotter to see in person than it is to read about. I shift in Jafar's lap, rubbing my thighs together. His cock is a hard length against my ass, but he simply keeps me in the gentle cage of his arms. His thumb idly strokes the underside of my breast, and he plays the fingers of his other hand across the sensitive skin of my thigh. Close to where I ache for him. So close.

I wonder if he'll touch me if I answer his question.

What's going on in my head?

I wish I knew.

I wasn't prepared for this. That truth becomes clearer every second I spend in this place. I've read about these things, fantasized about them, come more times than I can count to those very fantasies. But seeing in person? It feels like standing in the middle of a hurricane, each gust of wind tearing away a piece of the wall I spent my entire life building up around me.

The only thing steady is the man at my back, and if that's not the very definition of irony, I'm not sure what is. *He's* the reason I'm in this situation to begin with, adrift with no compass and no map, completely helpless in the face of the elements.

I take a deep breath and a leap of faith. "I like that he's on display."

"Watching or fantasizing about being in his place?" Jafar dips his hand farther beneath my dress and draws a single finger over my pussy.

"Both." I part my legs. I can't help it. I want him to touch me, and I don't care that people might see.

Or maybe the fact that people might watch only adds to the lust filling me to the brim and beyond.

"Wicked girl." He keeps up that gentle touch, torturing me with need. "You want that pretty little cunt on display. You know damn well that anyone who looks at you will want a taste." He nips my earlobe, the sharp pain making me gasp and squirm against him. "Just for that, I should let them. Blindfold you and put you in a spreader bar so you can't play the bashful virgin." Another stroke of that evil finger, this time directly over my clit. "I'll let them eat your pussy until you're begging for mercy, and then I'll fuck you right there in front of them to remind everyone—to remind *you*—of who you belong to."

I shouldn't want exactly what he's describing.

Except, no. That's not me talking. That's the shame I've had drilled into my head since before I could speak. Good girls do this. Girl girls don't do that.

Good girls don't want their pussies licked by strangers.

Good girls certainly don't want to be claimed in the most

intimate and public way possible by a man who's supposed to be the enemy.

Fuck. That.

I relax against Jafar, inch by torturous inch. I let my legs drape on either side of his thighs, let him have full access to my body. The dress still hides anything too intimate from view, but it's not about that. It's about accepting what I want without "shouldn't" involved. "Is that supposed to be a punishment or a reward?"

His deep laugh startles me. Have I ever actually heard him laugh before? Jafar drags his mouth over my bare shoulder. "That answers my question. Another night, baby girl, and we'll see how you can earn that experience."

I shiver. So many experiences I want, so many I don't have enough information to know I want.

A group of people walk through the door, and a man peels away from them to head in our direction. Jafar murmurs in my ear, "Remember the rules."

Eyes down. Silence.

As if I can find words with him pushing two fingers into me. I tense, waiting for him to withdraw his hand at the man takes the chair across from us. Jafar doesn't. He just keeps fucking me slowly with his fingers.

My dress covers me, yes, but the slinky fabric hides nothing of the movement of Jafar's hand. There is absolutely no question to what he's doing to me. I don't know what I expect, but the man glances down, grins, and slouches back in his chair as if he has conversations with couples in the midst of finger fucking every day. Who knows? Perhaps he does.

"Jafar."

"Hook."

I try to concentrate on what they're saying, but Jafar pushes a third finger into me and then starts slowly circling my clit with his thumb. I let my head fall back against his shoulder and focus on keeping my moans from escaping. If he doesn't stop, I'm going to come right here in front of this stranger, and that knowledge only makes my pleasure spike hotter.

I writhe, but Jafar shifts his free hand to band across my stomach, holding me still as he pushes me closer and closer to the edge. If not for his hard cock against my ass, I wouldn't have any indication that he's affected by what he's doing to me. His dry tone as he speaks with Hook certainly doesn't give anything away.

He increases the pressure and that's all I need. My orgasm bows my back and I grip his wrist as I ride his hand, unable to stop myself from grinding down against his fingers, soaking up every bit of pleasure he gives me.

Hook booms out a laugh. "Christ, Jafar, why are you wasting time talking with me when you have her willing to ride you like that?"

"Business first, Hook. Always."

I open my eyes to find Hook watching me. Watching us. His expression is a little mean, but it reeks of jealousy rather than anything as simple as enmity. He pushes to his feet and his fitted pants don't hide the fact that he enjoyed the show. He catches my look and grins. "You get bored with this asshole, you're more than welcome to come play with me."

Meg is more compelling than any single person has right to be. Hades scares me a little, because I'm sure his charm covers up unplumbed danger, but he's just as compelling in his own way. Hook is attractive enough. He's built lean in a way that makes me think of a sword—one wrong move and an enemy won't even feel the cut until they're bleeding out on the floor. Just business, and in that way he's likely no different from Jafar.

The difference is that Jafar cares about me enough not to

want to break me open for his pleasure. To Hook, I'm simply a curiosity and I have no doubt he'd be careless with me. Again, nothing personal, but he wouldn't stick around long enough to ensure I *wasn't* bleeding out on the floor from a wound, imagined or otherwise.

Jafar slips his hand free of my dress and presses his fingers to my lips. I instinctively suck them deep, one at a time, tasting myself on his touch. He chuckles when Hook groans and palms the front of his pants. "She's taken, Hook. Find your own."

"Too many choices to tie myself down with one." He grins and then tips a mocking bow to us. "See you around, Jafar. I trust you won't go back on your word with me the same way you did with Balthazar."

There's nothing in Jafar's voice to indicate the way he tensed beneath me. "Don't cross me and my word is as good as yours."

"That's what I'm afraid of." Another of those booming laughs and he ambles away.

Jafar kisses my temple. "What did you think of our friend Hook?"

Is that a trick question? How was I supposed to concentrate on anything at all with him touching me like that? I think back, trying to come up with something. "He's afraid you're going to attempt to expand your territory and he's worried he can't hold his."

"What makes you say that?" As always, his tone gives nothing away. He could be asking about the weather for all the interest he shows.

I know better by now. "If he was confident, he wouldn't feel the need to seek you out. He'd make preparations to hold his territory—he'd be a fool not to—but he'd keep all word of those preparations to himself so he'd have a chance at surprising you."

"Well done." He sets me on my feet and straightens my dress. "Are you ready for your reward?"

I'm still reeling from the balloon of warmth in my chest that his praise brought into existence. I barely manage to keep from pressing my hand to the spot between my breasts, sure that if I do I'll feel the physical evidence of the change in temperature there. I lick my lips. "Uh … Yes. Yes, I'm ready for my reward."

He doesn't stand immediately. He just watches me with a strange look on his face, as if he can't decide whether to be proud of me or to do something to put me in my place. I find myself holding my breath, waiting to see which side of the line he falls on.

This whole thing.

Everything. My life now. The room behind me, filled with people in various stages of pain and pleasure. The man sitting before me.

I thought I was prepared. I spent years reading everything I could get my hands on. The romance novels, yes, but also tomes of nonfiction on everything from current politics to gardening to law and contracts. I always planned to escape. The timing never felt right. No, that's not correct. It had nothing to do with timing and everything to do with my courage failing me before I could take that first step. Tonight reinforces that lack of courage. I can fake it with the best of them, but the truth is that I'm terrified. If I walked into this place without Jafar's hand on my back, I would have turn and fled. The sheer number of people is sensory overload enough.

It's not until he stands and pulls me against his chest that I realize I'm shaking. Weak. So incredibly weak when all I want is to be strong. I close my eyes and let my forehead rest against his shoulder for a beat, two. On the third, I raise my head and try to push away.

"Not yet." His hand is at the back of my neck again, his favorite spot. He easily holds me to him.

To be honest, I don't fight that hard.

"I want this." This. The sex. The life outside my father's walls. The freedom I can't quite seem to wrap my mind around. "Why am I struggling?"

"Learn to crawl before you start sprinting."

He said something to that nature before, but I barely paid attention to it. I'm paying attention now. I fight against the despair threatening to steal my breath. I am strong. I *am*. It doesn't matter that I don't feel strong in this moment, that if he wasn't here to hold me up, I might fall to my knees and never get up. I close my eyes, ashamed of the way they burn. "I don't know how to do that." I don't know how to do any of it, and that knowledge stings just as much as the tears I refuse to allow to fall.

"I'll show you." He takes my hand and tugs me toward the back of the room.

I dig in my heels out of instinct, but as often as Jafar and I are at each other's throats, he hasn't done anything tonight except keep me on my feet. Yes, I know being here serves his ultimate purpose and that he's showing me off like a prize for a conquering king, but it doesn't change the fact that he's been startlingly careful with me.

I can trust him this far, can't I?

I keep my gaze pinned to the middle of his back as he navigates the room. It's full of significantly more people than when we first arrived. I get flashes of men and women of every age, shape, and color engaged in various sexual and painful displays. Some of them seem to just be here for the conversation, though impossible to miss the way most have someone kneeling at their side. Eyes downcast. Silent.

Jafar's not the only one who extends those rules, apparently.

He stops in front of yet another door, though this one doesn't have anyone guarding it. As soon as we step through, quiet descends and I breathe out a sigh of relief, some of the tension bleeding out of my body. I can do this. Whatever *this* is.

Doors line the hallway, and it takes me several steps before I realize what's strange about the walls. "They're mirrors?"

"No." He pulls me toward a section of the hallway bathed in light and I finally understand. The wall isn't a mirror.

It's a window.

There are two women in the room. One is an icy blonde so beautiful that it almost hurts to look at her. The other is dark haired, but I can't see her face because it's buried between the blonde's spread legs. "Oh." I take in the cuffs holding the brunette's arms captive behind her back. Her bare back is red and I realize why as the blonde brings a flogger down across her skin. The blonde lifts her gaze and meets mine, the sheer strength behind it driving me back a step.

"*Oh.*" I press my hand to my lips. "Do they …"

"Yes, they like being watched, and yes, they like knowing they're being watched." He doesn't give me more opportunity to watch before pulling me several doors down. I catch sight of a discrete green light above the handle and then Jafar opens the door and tugs me into the room.

Lights flip on the second we step inside. I'm not sure what I expected, but it's a relatively normal looking bedroom. Jafar clears his throat, and I drag my attention to him. He points to a series of switches next to the door. "You control the transparency of the wall here." His finger moves to the red button. "Panic button. It will bring Hades's people running." He points to a camera tucked into the corner of the room. "Once your membership passes the three-month mark, you have the option of turning off the camera while you play."

"My membership."

His lips quirk. "Starts tonight."

A lot of information to process, but I allow it to slide away for when I'm alone. Right now, it's easier to focus on Jafar and what he expects of me. To anticipate my reward.

He leans against the wall and crosses his arms over his chest. "Your reward, your choice, baby girl. How do you want to play this?"

I open my mouth to tell him that he's ruining the fantasy, but it's not the truth. He's giving me a choice, a clear choice. He has been since the beginning, even if it suited my purposes to pretend otherwise. Part of me still wants to push him, to make him choose so I don't have to. The rest of me knows Jafar won't let me get away with that. I lick my lips, gathering the shreds of my courage. "Make me, Daddy."

His dark eyes flare hot enough to scald me to the core, but he doesn't move. "Remind me of your safe word."

Remind *myself*, he means. "Rajah," I whisper. The thrill I get out of the fight, out of telling him no, is unparalleled, but it only works if there's no miscommunication between us. I know that. I've always known that.

I take a step back and he pushes off the wall, stalking toward me. My heart leaps in fear and desire. Yes, this. This is what I need. Him chasing me down and fucking me back to safe ground. I step out of my heels and pick up my skirt so I won't trip on it. There isn't much space to maneuver in this room. I have to get the bed between us.

I bolt right as he grabs for me. He catches my skirt and yanks me back a step, but I'm not going down so quickly. I jerk away, ripping the fragile fabric. The sound only makes me hotter. Wetter.

He sees it. Of course he sees it. His grin is nearly feral. "I'm going to rip that dress right off your body."

"You're going to try." I scramble back to the edge of the bed, only then realizing what a poor plan this was.

Or a brilliant one.

He's on me before I reach the corner of the mattress. Instead of tackling me, Jafar hooks an arm around my waist and tosses me onto the bed. I land and flop onto my back, aiming a kick at his head. He laughs. The bastard *laughs*. I kick out again, and this time I make contact right in the center of his chest.

Too late, I realize he allows it.

CHAPTER 11

JASMINE

*J*afar grabs me behind my knees and drags me to the edge of the bed. I fight, need spiking every time he overpowers me. He flips me onto my stomach and jerks me half off the bed so my toes barely touch the ground. He kicks my feet wide and steps between my thighs before I can close them. I curse and wriggle, but he's got me pinned by the back of the neck before I can move an inch. "Sloppy, baby girl. You gave me more of a fight last time."

"Fuck you!"

He rips my dress up the back, baring me from the waist down, and delivers a stinging slap to first one cheek and then the other. "The proper response is 'Fuck you, Daddy.'"

"Fuck you, *Daddy*." It doesn't come out as sharp as I'd like. Instead, it's dangerously close to a moan. In my current position, I'm helpless. I can't touch the floor enough to leverage myself away, not with my legs spread like this. Not with his hand on the back of my neck, pressing down just enough that I can't escape.

"You've been bad, baby girl." He delivers another stinging

slap to my ass, the spike of pain shooting directly to my clit. "I should put you over my knee for that alone."

"You wouldn't dare!" *Do it.*

His dark laugh is my only answer. "You keep telling me no, but your pussy is telling me yes." He shoves two fingers into me, not easing me into it. I cry out. I can't help it. Just like I can't help spreading my legs wider yet and arching my back to offer myself to him. To allow him deeper. His thumb presses against my ass, a pressure that makes me freeze on instinct. "Do you know what I thought about when I saw you walking in the halls of your father's house?"

Oh god.

"I don't want to know." I should have realized how it would go when I decided on playing this way, should have anticipated. I shove hard against the mattress, but he easily keeps me pinned in place, his low voice stripping me bare even as his fingers possess me in the most intimate way possible.

"How many times did we talk, baby girl? Every time you pretended you weren't seeking me out, that this isn't what you wanted."

"No. I didn't want this." *Yes, yes, I did.*

He still hasn't moved his hand, still hasn't done anything but apply more pressure to my ass. "You were asking for it."

"No!"

"Yes." He pushes a third finger into me. "Every time you had to get the last word, every time you walked away from me and twitched that ass in my direction, this is what you wanted."

"Liar."

His low chuckle has my toes curling. Just like that, he withdraws his fingers, and I can't help a whimper of protest. Jafar steps closer to the bed and then I can feel his cock through his slacks. His weight presses me down against the mattress almost, *almost*, giving my clit enough friction. "Who's the real liar, baby girl? You know what I think? I think you wanted me to drag you into his office. To shove up your skirt and rip off your panties."

"No," I whisper. I can't help it. I writhe, my hips seeking the friction I need to get off.

He shoves a hand between me and the mattress, the touch against my clit nearly sending me over the edge. But he doesn't move, doesn't apply the pressure I need. The new position puts his lips directly against my ear, and I can feel his words rumbling through his chest against my back. "You want me to take it, to bend his virgin daughter over his desk and shove my cock into her tight little cunt. That way you don't have to admit it. You can still be a good girl instead of the little slut we know you are."

I gasp, my body going so tight, I might orgasm from his words alone. I almost moan before I remember the game. It takes me two tries to wet my throat enough to find words. "I *am* a good girl."

"You, baby girl, are a little slut." He nips my earlobe. "You know how I know that?"

"How?" I whisper.

"I know that because you're so desperate to grind against my fingers, your pussy is drenched. You want me to do it, to force you so you can keep pretending when we both know the truth."

I roll my hips, the pressure of his fingers making me bite my bottom lip hard. "What's the truth?"

"That I can fuck your mouth, your pussy, your ass, and you'll love every second of it." Another nip to my earlobe. "That I can pull three people in here at random and let them fuck you however they feel like and even as you tell yourself you don't want it, that I took away your choice, you'll come again and again, and keep lifting your hips in invitation for more. That you can't get enough."

I lose my battle of resistance. I writhe, grinding against his fingers. "You wouldn't dare."

"Meg will love licking that pretty pussy of yours. She'll love doing it even more while you ride Hook's cock and another man fucks your mouth."

I don't know who those people are, not really. They're strangers to me. It doesn't seem to matter. All I can do is imagine two cocks filling me, another mouth on my clit and Jafar watching it all. *Directing* it all. I fist the comforter and roll my hips harder, trying to find the right angle. His hand shifts beneath me and I freeze as he pinches my clit. Hard.

"So wanton." The devil is Jafar's voice in my ear, full of sin and promised pleasure. It might cost me my soul, but what is a soul in comparison with a night's pleasure? Just like that, the weight of him is gone. I press my forehead to the bed and work up the energy to stand. By the time I turn around, he's composed himself. As if he wasn't just spinning out a fantasy so dirty, I'm shaking just from imagining it. He considers me. "You want to be forced, but the flavor is wrong."

What's he talking about?

My heart takes up residence in my throat, each beat pressing against the sensitive skin there and leaving me dizzy. "What?"

But he's already moving to the door. "Stay here. This will only take a minute."

For a moment, I think he's joking, but he leaves the room, the door clicking shut softly behind him. I sink onto the bed and stare down at my torn dress. I was ready. I *am* ready. My body craves his with a strength that leaves me fighting not to chase him through the halls of this place and beg for the denied orgasm. To beg for his cock. I have nothing left but my pride at this point, so I force myself still.

It's only when the door opens again that I realize I was really forcing myself to obey.

Except it's not Jafar who walks into the room.

I blink. "Tink?"

"The one and only." She shuts the door and turns, which is when I get a good look at what she's wearing. Or, really, what she's not. A lace slip hugs her curves, barely covering her breasts and ass, held only in place because it has garters on the side attached to thigh-highs. It's sexy, but that's not what has me fighting not to stare.

She's not wearing anything underneath.

She smirks at me. "For someone who put on a cute little show out in the main room, you're awfully easy to shock."

"You saw that?"

"Princess, *everyone* saw that." She tosses several articles of clothing onto the bed next to me. "Jafar wants you to put these on and follow me."

Questions bubble up to press against the inside of my lips, but I keep them inside. I have a feeling Tink won't tell me. More than that, I either trust Jafar in this place or I don't. I cautiously lift the plaid skirt. *Oh.*

"Schoolgirl is sexy, I'm not even going to lie." Tink pauses. "Do you want me to turn around?"

"Why? You've seen everything." I stand on shaking legs and strip out of the red dress. The clothing is missing a few essential items—namely a bra—but I'm surprised to find white panties included. I expect cotton, but this is a lace thong that is just as minuscule as the skirt. I pull on the panties and skirt, which barely covers my ass. The shirt, however, gives me trouble. "I don't ..."

"Here." Tink brushes my hands to the side, undoes the buttons I've been struggling with, and ties it under my breasts instead. She steps back and shakes her head. "Yeah, you look hot for teacher. Wait, one more thing." She pulls a hair tie off her wrist and moves around behind me. "This is easier if you kneel."

I obey without thinking and wait as she pulls my hair back into a tight ponytail. Tink squeezes my shoulder. "Check yourself out, princess."

I stand and walk to the mirror and ... "Wow." I can see my dark nipples through the thin fabric of the white shirt and tying it up has left a large swathe of my stomach barred. The skirt looks even tinier than it feels, and as I move experimentally, I flash white panties. I turn around and, yes, the lower curve of my ass is clearly visible. "I look indecent."

"That's kind of the point." She moves to the door. "Come on. He's waiting."

I know what fantasy we're playing out now. It's not a school teacher like Tink thinks. It's the one Jafar growled into my ear in this very room. I have to fight not to clench my thighs together as I follow Tink out of the room. She leads me farther down the hall and points to a door. "This one." She grins. "Have fun, princess."

I carefully open the door and step into the room. Shock has my feet growing roots and my fingers going slack to release the door. The room looks like a gentleman's office. Thick carpet beneath my feet. One wall lined with books and the other containing several framed landscape prints. Leather chairs sit opposite a massive mahogany desk that's polished until it shines. A single lamp in the corner offers little in the way of illumination. It's not an exact match to my father's office, but it's close enough to evoke the feeling I always got when I was called there.

Shame. Anger. Fear.

I clench my hands and press back against the cool wood of the door. It's just a room, but Jafar choosing this one ... Oh yes, he definitely did it on purpose. Movement has me lifting my head. He's there in the shadows of the room, leaning against the wall behind the desk. How many times did Jafar stand exactly there when my father doled out his punishments for my misbehavior? More times than I can count.

As if sensing my thoughts, he says, "You've been bad, baby girl." He pushes off the wall, but doesn't move from his spot. "Willfully disobedient. Mouthy."

My body can't tell if I'm turned on or terrified. I clench my hands at my sides and try not to shake. "I'm sorry, Daddy. I won't do it again."

"I wasn't finished." His mild words have my snapping my mouth shut to keep from babbling. He finally takes a step forward, into the light. His expression is so cold, it stings me from across the room. "Look at you. You're dressed like a little slut and you've been walking around like that, teasing the men."

My nipples go tight and my panties damp. As much as part of me wants to obey him, to beg for forgiveness, I have never submitted without a fight, and I'm not about to start now. "I like my clothes."

"You like your clothes." He shakes his head slowly, his gaze raking over me. The ice in his expression cracks for half a second, letting me see the inferno beneath, before he regains control of himself. "You're getting off on leading them around by their dicks, showing them what they want but they can never have."

I lift my chin. "Who says they can't have it?"

Something dangerous flickers through his eyes, and I shiver. "Put your hands on the desk."

"No."

He starts toward me. Slow and as unstoppable as the tide. Instinct takes over and I run. There's nowhere to go, though. He catches me by my hair before I've taken three steps. Pain brings tears to my eyes, or maybe it's a delicious kind of shame. Either way, he wraps my hair around his fist and uses that hold to steer me to the desk. "Don't make me ask again."

"Yes, Daddy," I grit out. I slap my hands on the desk, petulance in every move.

Just like that, he releases my hair. "Have you let them do more than look, baby girl? Have they slipped their fingers up this little tease of a skirt and touched you through your panties?" His voice lowers. "Have they gone so far as to tug your panties to the side to see you?"

This might be fantasy, but it *feels* real. "No, of course not. I'm a good girl."

"Liar." His broad hand presses against the middle of my back, bending me until my cheek is pressed against the cool wood of the desk. The new position has my skirt hiked up to the top of my ass, baring me. Jafar tsks. "Look at that. You're just asking to be fucked."

"No, I'm not."

"Not asking. *Begging*." His hands drop to my ass, squeezing me, parting me. "Are your panties damp because you like giving them a show? Or because you let them touch what's mine?"

I don't know what the right answer is. I can't think, can't move, can only focus on keeping still and not rolling my hips in invitation to touch me. "I'm sorry, Daddy," I whisper. I'm not even sure what I'm apologizing for.

"That answers my question, doesn't it?" He runs a finger under the band of my thong and down the back, pulling the lace away from my body. Shame suffuses me as he reaches the front, as he finds out how wet they are. His sound of disappointment lances through me. "I try to keep you safe for your own good. But if you're so determined to throw that back in my face, then I'll give you exactly what you're begging for."

I try to push off the desk, but he's expecting me. One

hand grips the nape of my neck, and the other drags my panties to the side. "Look at you." Despite the controlled violence of his moves, his voice is just as mild as ever. It's so fucking hot, I can barely stand it. He drags a finger across my pussy and bends over me to hold the evidence of my desire in front of my face. "Wet and wanton," he says.

"I just like them looking. I don't want them to touch. I was never going to let them touch me." I don't know where the words come from, but they pour out into the air between us. "Please, Daddy. Please don't punish me."

"You think you can walk around in that little skirt, your pussy drenched and begging for it, and not pay the consequences? Baby girl, you know better."

He releases me, and I shove up, my instincts demanding I run. Jafar is ready for me, of course. He allows me to turn and then he's there, bodily lifting me onto the desk and stepping between my thighs even as I try to fight him. "Ah ah." He catches my chin in a punishing grip. His gaze drops to my mouth and for one breathless moment, I'm sure he'll kiss me. Instead, he shifts his hand to my ponytail, using it to force me to look down my body. "You're a liar on top of being a little slut." He drags a single finger down the edge of my shirt. It shifts to the side to bare my nipple. "No bra. Panties that show your pussy as much as they hide them." He sounds almost sad. *Disappointed.* "I treat you like a princess, and this is how you repay me."

"I'm sorry, Daddy. I promise I'll be good." But I can't stop myself from arching my back to expose my breast further.

He slaps my nipple, the sharp pain sending me writhing. Jafar shakes his head. "You want to be fucked like a little slut, baby girl. So be it." He holds me immobile and yanks my shirt to the side. The knot holds, the tightness of the fabric offering up my breasts to his gaze. His tsks again and forces me back a few inches to drag up my skirt and hook his fingers around my panties. I try to fight him, but he's too strong. He drags them down my legs one inch at a time and then tosses them away. "Spread your thighs."

I clench them together. "No."

"Yes." If anything, his tone gets gentler, a direct counterpoint to the pain of his grip on my hair. He cups one breast and circles my nipple with his thumb. "Spread your thighs and let Daddy give you a kiss."

A shiver works its way through my whole body. I want to keep struggling, but I want his mouth on me even more. Still, I hesitate. "I want to be good."

"No, you don't." His voice still has a sliver of disappointment in it, but he's stopped hiding the dark desire written across his face. Like I'm being bad, and he's allowing it, but it's turning him on despite himself. I *know* it's just play, but power still sizzles through me, driving my desire higher.

I lean back on my hands and spread my thighs. Slowly, tentatively. I want what he's offering, but the shame I feel isn't totally feigned. This man is supposed to be my enemy, but I'm starting to fear I'll do anything he asks as long as he keeps drawing forth my darkest desires and putting them into action.

He releases my hair and steps back, taking me in. Jafar's gaze drags over my pussy, heavy and hot. "Wider." I obey faster this time, and he chuckles darkly. "This is what you wanted, isn't it? To force my hand." He goes to his knees in front of me and jerks my hips to the very edge of the desk. "You're practically dripping. It would be a shame for any of you to go to waste." He drags his tongue up my center and I can't stop myself from crying out.

Jafar leans back and slaps my clit. "None of that." His expression goes forbidding. "My men can't be walking around with cockstands for a pussy that isn't theirs. It belongs to me and me alone, do you understand?"

I wet my lips. "Yes, Daddy."

"I'm not a cruel man. I won't have you moaning and screaming and tempting them to taste you just like I am now." He grips my thighs hard enough to bruise, wrenching them wider yet. "You make too much noise, and I stop. Do you understand?"

"Yes, Daddy. I'll be quiet. I promise." I can barely think straight as I look down my body at the tableau he's created. I look just as much the little slut as he'd described me. My breasts are out, my skirt hiked up around my waist, my pussy exposed and begging for him. As I hold my breath, he dips down and gives me a long lick, his gaze holding mine.

It's sinful and decadent and I never want it to stop.

Jafar wedges his hands under my ass and lifts me to his mouth the same way he did in the car. As if he can't get close enough, can't drive his tongue deep enough into me. As if he'll devour me whole.

I want it more than I've wanted anything in far too long.

If he consumes me entirely, maybe he can take my guilt, my shame, my fear.

He can take everything.

CHAPTER 12

JASMINE

I half expect Jafar to bring me to orgasm as quickly as he has the last two times. I really should know better by now. He never does the expected, and this moment is no exception. He explores my pussy with his mouth as if we have all the time in the world. It's all too easy to pretend that we're actually in my father's office. That he sent Jafar to deliver my punishment instead of doing it himself. That Jafar lost control and finally touched me.

That he's really going to fuck me on my father's desk.

I whimper and everything stops. Jafar lifts his eyebrows and shakes his head sadly. "I told you."

"Wait." I reach for him, trying to move his mouth back to where I need him, but he catches my wrists and forces them to meet at the small of my back. "Jafar, Daddy, *please.*"

But he ignores my pleading and stands slowly. I press my lips together, torn between being quiet and saying whatever it takes to get his mouth on me again. He gives me another of those long looks that seems like he can reach into my mind and draw forth every fantasy I've ever had. "You want to come?"

"Yes, please," I whisper.

"You want me to reward you for bad behavior."

"Yes." I shake my head. "No. I—I don't know."

He wraps his hand around my hair, and I know where we're headed even before he nudges me off the desk and guides me to my knees in front of him. I can't stop shaking, can't stop squirming as if the limited friction of my thighs is even close to enough to get me off. It's not, but it feels naughty to luxuriate in denied pleasure.

Jafar looks down his body at me, taking me in with dark eyes. He's still dressed to perfection, his suit barely rumpled from our struggles. His cock presses against his slacks and my mouth waters at being this close to doing something I've always wanted to do. He strokes a devastatingly gentle hand down my face. "You want to be a good girl? Prove it. Earn your reward."

I don't point out that sucking his cock is hardly *good girl* behavior. It doesn't matter. This is the game we play, and I love it. I undo his pants with shaking fingers and drag down the zipper. Seconds later, he's filling my hands. Long and broad and perfect. I'm too impatient to be cautious as I suck him down, reveling in the feeling of him filling me in a completely new way. His hand tightens on my hair, holding me back, but I fight the restraint and make a frustrated noise.

"Slow," he murmurs.

No.

I don't want slow and careful. I want rough and ready and everything he can give me. I dig my nails into his hips, pricking him the same way my frustration pricks me.

"Wicked girl." He shifts his grip, keeping one hand in my hair and tilting my head back a little. "You want me to fuck your mouth."

"Mmm."

He uses his free hand to touch my left wrist. "It's too much, you let me know."

I make another sound of assent. Jafar might like playing with the darker edge of desire the same way I crave, but he always manages to check in with me. To make sure I'm right there with him.

It makes me feel far safer than I have any right to.

He holds my head immobile as he begins to move. Slowly at first, testing my limits. I've never had a sensitive gag reflex, but it's not a trait I was particularly grateful for until the moment his cock bumps the back of my throat. It's not a comfortable feeling, but I breathe through my nose and relax into it as best I can. I want this.

I *need* this.

"That's it, baby girl." His soft praise lights me up from within, and I can't find the strength to hate the feeling. Instead, I luxuriate in it as he begins to move in earnest, thrusting between my lips, forcing me to relax into it or choke.

My eyes water and he wipes my tears away with a gentle thumb, so at odds with the rough hold on my hair. "Next time we do this, you're going to swallow me down. Every single fucking drop." He slams into me again and again, his voice low and rough and as brutal as the way he fucks my mouth. "But not tonight. Tonight I'm coming all over those tits you like flashing at everyone. Remind you who you belong to."

Once again, I'm left shaking and wondering if he can pull an orgasm from me with his words alone. Coming on my tits? It's dirty and a little degrading and I want it more than anything in that moment.

He wrenches me off his cock and fists it with his free hand, jerking himself once, twice, a third time. He comes in great spurts that lash my skin, the almost-agony on his face turning me on as much as his marking me does.

His shuddering exhale is the only warning I get before he releases me and steps back. I'm left swaying on my knees as he tucks his cock back into his pants and looks down at me. "You love this shit."

To fight or to embrace the truth?

I meet his gaze. "I love this shit, Daddy."

He pulls me to my feet, and then his mouth is on mine and nothing else matters. Claiming me with teeth and tongue, marking me as his with this searing kiss the same way he has with his mouth and hands and cock and come.

Jafar owns me, body and soul.

I'm too drunk on pleasure to fear that truth. Not tonight. There's plenty of time to let it sink in, to worry about the future tomorrow.

When he finally lifts his head, I have to cling to him to keep my feet. From his indulgent smile, he knows it. "Tell me how you want it."

No question to his meaning, not with his cock already going hard again. I almost tell him to bend me over the desk, but that's not the answer I give. "I want to ride you." He's some kind of wizard to pull the truth from me again and again, even when it would serve me better to lie.

He moves to one of the low leather chairs and sinks onto it with a grace I envy. As I watch, he undoes his pants and pulls his cock out. "Come take your reward, baby girl. You've more than earned it."

I unknot my shirt with fumbling fingers and shrug out of it. I'm still sticky with him, but I don't care. I'm not ready to wipe the mark away. After a hesitation, I slide out of the skirt, too.

I like the sexy outfit, but there's something particularly decadent about climbing into his lap while he's mostly fully clothed and I'm completely naked. I feel like the little slut he's named me, like he can do whatever he wants to me and I'll love every second of it. I've been captive too long. If I can't embrace the rest of the world, I'll embrace the endless variety that fucking brings.

This is just another flavor of it.

I'm so wet, I'm practically dripping. Jafar drapes his arms over the back of the chair, leaving me to guide this play. I'm not in charge, though. I'm a fool if I believe otherwise.

I guide his cock into me and sink down until he's sheathed to the hilt. Even with the earlier orgasms and his fingers readying me half the night, it's still an adjustment. I roll my hips experimentally, shifting as the almost-pain of him melts into pure pleasure. "Oh."

"Mmm." His gaze tracks every flicker of my expression, reading me. "This is *my* fantasy, baby girl."

I blink. "What?"

"That I'm working late. The house is quiet around us, everyone off doing their own shit. And you walk through the door wearing nothing but that cocktease of a robe. We don't need to talk. You just drop the robe, climb into my lap, and take my cock just like this." He cups my breasts roughly, tugging at my nipples. "You don't even lock the door. You're too eager to get me inside you."

I brace my hands on his shoulders and lift myself almost all the way off his cock, only to slide down again and take him deeper yet. I roll my hips, rocking against him. Yes, this is exactly what I need. "I need your cock too much to worry about someone walking in."

"You have my cock." The way he says it almost sounds like he means something else, but desire wraps too tightly around us for me to divine what.

I rock faster, my orgasm building with every stroke. "I want them to walk in." I can't stop fucking him, can't stop talking, simply can't stop. "I want them to watch me ride your cock, to see you slide into my body, to see you claim me." So many things I shouldn't want, but I burned *shouldn't* to ash tonight. I don't care what a good girl would want, because I *do* want these things.

And Jafar seems only too happy to provide them.

"You want them to watch." His voice is so low, it rumbles through my body in the most delicious of ways. He finally touches me, grasping my chin and bringing my gaze to him. "That's just for starters. Yes, they'll watch. They'll fist their cocks and imagine it's *them* you're so desperate for." He pulls me closer yet, until his wicked promises ghost against my lips. "And next time, I'll crook my finger and one of them will join. We'll pass you around just like you're craving, let you fuck us until you run out of desire."

I can't breathe.

Every time he mentions the idea of more people in the room, more people *inside me*, I can barely process the sheer need that rolls through me. "My mouth?" I breathe.

"Mouth. Cunt." His other hand moves down to trace my crack. "Ass." His slow grin has me grinding harder on him, fighting to take his cock deeper yet. "But not tonight. Tonight is just for watching."

He releases my ass and reaches behind him. I'm still trying to figure out what he's doing when he uses his grip on my chin to turn my head to the wall bordering the hallway.

It's completely transparent now, and there's a crowd watching. Men and women, both. I pick out Meg near the front. She meets my gaze and smiles slowly, sending a bolt of sheer heat through me. "Oh, god."

"This is what you wanted."

Not a question, but demanding an answer all the same. "Yes, Daddy."

He pulls me off his cock and rearranges us, moving to

bend me over the chair. He pulls the tie out of my hair and then digs his fist into it, using the hold to turn my face to look at the clear window.

And then he's shoving inside me, somehow so much deeper than when I rode him. "Don't close your eyes. Watch them and know that they'd give damn near anything to be in here with us."

Yes.

I keep a white knuckled grip on the back of the chair as he slams into me. I look at the people watching. I can't help it. I don't want to.

Lust. So much lust, I could drown in it. They're watching me and I know the angle has our bodies in profile. They can see his cock sliding into my pussy, can see my breasts bounce with every stroke, can see my wetness coating my thighs.

Yes, yes, yes.

"Touch that greedy little clit of yours. I want you coming around my cock. Put on a show, baby girl. I know how much you crave being the center of attention."

I have to shift to brace my hand on the seat of the cushion and the new position leaves my ass in the air like an offering Jafar is only too happy to take advantage of. As I circle my clit, he does something that changes the angle and I can't help but cry out. "Yes, Daddy!"

He does it again, working that one spot inside me while I work my clit. I want to last, to draw out the show, to keep this forbidden feeling going longer. It's too good. Too perfect.

I tumble over the edge, Jafar's name on my lips as oblivion reaches up and sucks me under.

* * *

I MUST DRIFT off at some point after Jafar cleans us up and

wraps me in a warm blanket in his lap, because I wake in an unfamiliar room alone. I sit up and stretch, smiling at the ache in my body. The earlier nerves of being in this place are long gone, chased away by the grounding effect Jafar has on me. Foolish to trust him enough for that, even more foolish to let him draw me back to earth one rough stroke at a time. I'm not sure what other option I have.

I agreed to play his game the moment I ran from him.

I don't see how to win this, though. He holds all the cards, and the only advantage I have is that he wants me. That's it. A poor advantage as such things go. Jafar isn't one to lose his head and let his cock take control.

The door opens and my heart actually skips a beat. He's back.

Except the man who steps out of the shadows isn't Jafar.

It's Ali.

I yank the sheet up to clutch against my chest. "What are you doing here?"

He grins. Ali has a rakish short of charm that dazzled my father. It doesn't dazzle me. No one else seems to notice or care that his smiles never reach his black eyes. That there's a mean glint there that raises the small hairs on the back of my neck every time I'm in the same room as him. That, from the moment we met, he looked at me like he owned me.

And now I'm *naked* in a room with him.

"Ali, what are you doing here?" Surely he's not a member? If he was, Jafar would have said something. I glance past him to the door, and he laughs.

"He's busy. We have a few minutes." He moves closer, but stops when I jerk back. His mop of curly hair might be charming on another man, and his slow smile certainly would be. But this isn't another man. This is *Ali*. "Jasmine, I'm going to save you."

I blink. "What?"

"He killed your father. Did you know that?" He takes another step. He's nearly to the bed. "Took him into your backyard and shot him like a dog that needed to be put down."

I know my father is dead, of course. I won't mourn that man. I refuse to.

But I don't know how I feel about this apparent execution Ali describes. "Please leave."

"You're right. No way can I get you out of here with all of Hades's people around." He reaches out, startlingly fast, and grabs my hand. I lose my grip on the sheet and it falls to my waist. Ali stares at my breasts for a long moment and I stare back, refusing to fight him despite the fear leaving me cold. I'm afraid of what he might do if I try to pull my hand back.

Playing that way with Jafar is one thing. *Play*. It might not look like it to an observer, but I know the truth.

Ali isn't Jafar. This isn't play. I want to shower off the filthy way he makes me feel with a single look. Fear clogs my throat, slowing my thoughts. A scream builds in my throat, a sound full of terror and rage. It leaves me hoarse from the fight not to set it free. "He'll be back soon."

I mean it as a threat. Jafar will kill Ali. Even if he didn't intend to before now, if he walks in on this scene, I have no doubt how he'll react. *He* won't misread the situation.

Ali takes it another way. "You're right." He drops my hand. "Be ready, Jazz. I'm going to get you out." He lunges forward and takes my mouth in a brutal kiss that sends shards of ice tearing through me. "Until then." He's up and out of the room before I can react.

I stare at the door until I'm sure he won't return. Only then does my stomach lurch sickeningly. I scramble off the bed and through the open door to the small bathroom, barely making it to the toilet in time to be sick. I retch again and again, unable to stop feeling his mouth against mine. A promise that's nothing more than a threat.

He wants me for the same reason Jafar wants me—a trophy in their game of tug-a-war. An outward representation of the power they claimed. Or, rather, the power Ali *wants* to claim.

"Jasmine?"

I tense for half a second before I register Jafar's rumbling voice. *Not* Ali.

And then he's there, crouching next to me. "Jasmine, are you okay?" Jafar reaches out, but stops before he makes contact. "Did I hurt you?"

He thinks this reaction is about him.

About what we did earlier.

I might be smarter if I let him keep believing that, but I can't. I just can't. "No." Strangely enough, my stomach settles the second his big hand makes contact with my back. I draw in a shuddering breath. "No, it's not you. I'm fine. I …" A mistake to play my cards now, to let him know what Ali's plans are? No, I can't believe that. If I'm destined to be in a cage, better the one Jafar has crafted around me than anything Ali has to offer. He's no better than my father. *Worse* than my father because he wants to fuck me.

"Talk to me." The quiet command settles me further.

I slump back against the glass of the shower and close my eyes. Easier to speak if I can't see him. "Ali was here." I feel him go still, feel the rage rise in a tidal wave that can drown us both, but he waits for me to continue. I clear my throat. "He says he's decided to save me, but I think we both know that he only wants me because he thinks the power of my father's territory is tied up with who owns me."

"Your father's people need someone larger than life to follow and for all that they're killers, they have a romantic streak a mile wide. You're a beautiful counterpoint to any ill will the person at your side might bring to the table. They'll follow you—will follow whoever you're married to."

Married.

I open my eyes. "No one said anything about marriage."

"No one said anything about marriage." He nodded, never taking his gaze from my face. "Yet."

If I concentrate, I can almost feel the trap clamping shut around my leg. It's not enough to keep me locked up in his penthouse. Or to bring me here like some prized cow to show off before it's slaughtered.

Do I believe that what Jafar seems to feel for me is real? Yes. He might be a superb liar, but he's never bothered to with me. Do I think for a second that it will stop him from using me as he sees fit?

No. Absolutely not.

I draw my tattered pride around me as best I can and lift my chin. "I'm not marrying anyone, Jafar. Not him. Not you."

"We'll see, won't we?"

CHAPTER 13

JAFAR

*A*li was here.

He could have killed her. *Would* have if he didn't still think that he could salvage this coup. The thought of him hurting her makes my entire body go cold. I wasn't here and I should have been.

I wasn't fucking here.

He might not have injured her, but Ali did something to upset Jasmine enough that she's sick. Or she was. Right now, she's looking at me like she wants to rip my throat out for mentioning marriage. A stupid move on my part, a misstep I wouldn't have made if I was thinking clearly. But I saw her clinging to the toilet and all I could think of was that I'd broken what little trust we have between us. There's no coming back from that shit. I know that better than anyone. Jasmine and I already have a mountain of challenges in front of us without letting my cock get in the way of reason.

My cock always seems to get in the way of reason when it comes to this woman.

I want to stand to race out of the room and track down Hades to punch in his smug face for having shitty enough security to allow Ali into this building. It shouldn't be possible. *I* can't even sneak into The Underworld. I tried when I first arrived in Carver City, but the procedures in place are too thorough.

Which means Ali didn't sneak in.

Hades allowed him entrance.

Yes, the old bastard and I would have a conversation, and soon.

But not right now. Not with Jasmine sitting there, still shaking, her eyes too wide. I hold out my hand. "Come here." As much as I want to pick her up and just fucking take care of her, it will do more harm than good right now.

"I'm not marrying you."

I bite back a sigh. "A slip of the tongue, baby girl. It's not on the table."

"Not yet, but it will be."

She's not wrong. A marriage might not be enough to fully cement things, but it won't hurt. It also has the benefit of creating a narrative people can root for. No one wants to be ruled by a monster who went back on his word and killed the man he owed allegiance to. But a man in love, desperate to save his woman from an arranged marriage? That's a whole hell of a lot more romantic. That's something people can get behind and celebrate.

"Come here." I put a little sting into my words, and sure enough, that gets her moving. She places her hand in mine and allows me to pull her to her feet. I lift her onto the bathroom counter and run my hands over her body. "Did he hurt you?" There are bruises there, but they're caused by *my* hands and she came apart around my cock while I gave them to her. "Did he touch you?"

"Not the way you mean." She shivers and I open the narrow cabinet Hades keeps stocked in all the overnight rooms. It's filled with anything a person needs if they're unexpectedly staying, and I pull out a toothbrush, toothpaste, and a fluffy robe. After wrapping the latter around her and tucking it in tight to her skin, I tear through the toothbrush packaging and dole out the toothpaste.

She plucks it from my hand. "I can brush my own teeth."

"I'm aware." It doesn't change the fact that I want to take care of her. A foreign feeling. Yeah, I've had plenty of sex in the past, and unlike some of the assholes out there, I actually care if my partner is having a good time. That means fucking, but it also means aftercare.

This feels different.

Everything with Jasmine feels different.

I'm not prepared for the protectiveness that surges through me as she finishes brushing her teeth and slides off the counter. I want to wrap her up and snarl at anyone who gets close. I want to rip Ali's fucking head off. "Did he hurt you, baby girl?"

She hesitates like she's thinking about lying to me. Finally Jasmine runs an absent hand over her waves of dark hair. "He scared me." She lifts her gaze to mine. "He said you put my father down like a mad dog in our backyard."

The bastard had seen that?

I had to make an example of Balthazar. More, I *wanted* to. If the piece of shit had listened to me, had taken my guidance, none of this wouldn't have been necessary. At least not for a few more years, once I had my relationship with Jasmine solidified. Instead, Balthazar got greedy, and now here we are, dealing with the fallout.

"It wasn't quite so dramatic."

Jasmine sighs. "This whole thing was broken from the start." She steps into me, allowing me to wrap my arms around her, and rests her forehead against my chest. "You're not a good man, Jafar."

"I know." With everyone else, I can put on the charming

face and pretend to be other that what I am. Not with her. Never with her. She's always seen right to the heart of me. It's what damned both of us.

Because I see her, too.

I make myself release her, make myself take a step back. "If you need to leave …"

She blinks those big, brown eyes at me, a line appearing between her strong brows. "You gave me that option already. I know the caveats."

"I'll release your trust." I curse myself for being a thousand times a fool for offering. Her trust is the one thing that ensures her defiance will only go so far. Having her need me is a tether binding us together. I'm bastard enough to keep her. I know that. I knew that when I forced her hand with that bullshit deal the night I took her the first time. "You can leave the city if you want."

Jasmine gives me an unhappy smile. "We both know I'm not equipped to deal with the world. Not now. Not yet. This club was enough to have me locking up in sensory overload. Do you really think I'm capable of going out on my own?" She shook her head. "I believed I could when all I had was theory. Now I know better."

"You're underestimating yourself." Why the fuck am I trying to convince her to leave? What the hell is wrong with me?

She moves past me and into the bedroom. "Even if I am, even if I actually landed on my feet, Ali will track me down and bring me back. He's all but promised it. As you said, people want a figurehead, and I make a damn good one."

"That's not all of it."

"What are you talking about?"

"Ali wants you because you were promised to him." I should shut the fuck up right now, but she needs to understand. "But now that you're mine, he wants you even more. If he thinks he can't get to you, he'll do something unforgivable."

She gives me a long look. "You mean he'll kill me."

"He'll try. I won't let him touch you."

Jasmine considers me for one last moment and then opens the closet and considers the offerings. Just like the bathroom, Hades keeps the closets stocked with a wide range of sizes. She pulls out a silky pair of cream pants and a matching top. They're obviously pajamas, but they'll more than suit on the ride home. Once dressed, she turns to me. "I have no option but you, and we both know it. Not as things stand now."

It should make me happy that she's capitulating. It means less fighting so I can focus my energy on other things. It means I can keep Jasmine safe.

It means I can *keep* her.

But as I stand there and watch her put herself to rights, the wrongness of this situation nags at me. I want Jasmine. No shit, I want Jasmine. Until I had her, that was the only thing that mattered. Now?

I want her to choose me.

I almost laugh out loud at the idiocy of the thought. Jasmine might like the way she comes on my cock, but if all things were in balance, she'd walk away and never look back. She has her sights set on things outside this world we move in, and I'd be a monster to hold her to the shadows when she was obviously meant to walk in the sunshine.

I *am* a monster.

I shrug out of my jacket and wrap it around her. It's not that cold outside, but I like the sight of her in my clothes. A statement, yes, but for once, I don't give a fuck who might see. It settles something in my chest. "I have one thing to take care of and then we're leaving."

Her gaze sharpens. "You want to talk to Hades."

No point in lying to her. It doesn't even occur to me to try. "Ali shouldn't have been able to get past the security." I need to know if he's that good, or if Hades has his own reasons for letting the man in, and I need to know it soon. Jasmine's safety hangs in the balance.

She meets my gaze. "I'd like to come with you."

It's on the tip of my tongue to deny her. Ali got into the room, so I'm hardly going to leave her here, but I know for a fact that Meg and the other two women in Hades's inner circle wind down in the early mornings in the lounge. I don't trust anyone, but Hades and his people care about reputation above all else. Even if he'd playing two sides against the middle, he won't hand over someone under his protection.

He'll just pretend not to know anything about it after Ali snatches her.

Jasmine touches my arm. "I'll remember the rules."

Eyes down. Silent.

It should please me. She's taken to submission so goddamn naturally. But I can barely breathe past the jagged feeling in my throat. "No." The word seems to surprise her as much as it surprises me. I take her hand and place it in the crook of my arm. "No, this concerns you as much as it concerns me. More."

"Jafar." She finally looks up at me. Even with her expression intentionally smoothed out, there are marks of weariness around her eyes and the faintest tremble in where her fingers touch my arm. Ali was *in the room* with her, close enough to do or say something that left her physically sick. I can't think about that too hard or I'm going to lose my shit.

I should have been there.

I want to bundle her up, to do something to make her feel safe, to put her feet back on solid ground. It's not in my skillset. I destroy things. I don't protect them. I clear my throat. "I'm sorry I wasn't here."

She frowns at me as if she's never seen me before. "If he came through that door while you were in bed with me, he could have killed you."

As much as I wish I could say otherwise, when she and I are fucking, I'm so wrapped up in her, an elephant could stampede through the room and I'd be none the wiser. "It doesn't matter."

It does matter. She's mine to conquer, yes, but more importantly, she's mine to protect. "He won't get to you again."

For a second, I think she might fight me just for the sake of fighting. I can't blame her for the urge. A cornered animal will swipe out at friend and foe alike. I'm still not sure which I am for this woman. Both. Neither. I want to burn this new fucking uncertainty inside me to ash and let it blow away in the wind. It won't happen as long as I'm touching her, and leaving her alone in this moment isn't an option. She needs me. She might cut out her own tongue before she admits it, but it's the damn truth.

"Ready?"

She nods slowly. "I wish you hadn't torn my dress. It feels like visiting a king in my underwear."

"Baby girl, you *are* essentially in your underwear." I lean down and murmur in her ear. "And you loved it when I ripped your clothes off. It had you wet and begging for my cock before I had even touched your pussy."

She shivers. "I like what I like." As simple as that.

Fuck, but if ever there was a woman who could send me to my knees, it's this one.

"I'm going to spend a fortune in clothes on you." I chuckle. The sound feels strange in my throat. The impulse to laugh only seems to come to life around her. "It's worth it."

"I know," she says primly, once again the little queen. It makes me want to fuck that control right out of her. Again.

Not now. Not while there are enemies circling and I have no idea how deep the rot goes. "Let's go."

I don't usually stay overnight in The Underworld if I can help it, but I have these hallways memorized. A plan is only as good as its exit strategy, though I've trusted Hades up to this point to follow his own rules. Ali having access to the club isn't a direct violation of that, but his coming into an occupied room without an invitation, *touching* my baby girl without invitation …

I'll fucking kill him.

Unsurprisingly, it's Meg who meets us at the small elevator that leads up to Hades's office from this floor. She looks just as fresh this morning as she did last night, though she's changed clothes and hairstyles somewhere along the way. Now, she's in a pair of slacks and a button-down shirt that's barely buttoned, leaving a large swathe of skin exposed from her neck to her stomach. She smiles at us, though there's a coldness in her blue eyes that she usually masks. "You're headed in the wrong direction for the exit."

"We need to speak with Hades. Please." I could demand to see him, throw my weight around, but it'll only result in him pulling a power play just to prove he can. Dealing with Hades is a constant dance of dominance and power, and I only come out on top about half the time.

Today needs to be one of those times.

She gives us a long look. "He's expecting you."

I bet he is. I keep my hand covering Jasmine's as we follow Meg onto the elevator and head up a floor. She doesn't speak, which is just as well. Meg might be Hades's right hand, might run this place just as much as he does, but at the end of the day, *he* is the one who leads. Which means he's the one I need to deal with.

We step off the elevators and she motions for us to follow her to a set of large dark doors. They stretch from the floor nearly to the ceiling, and the shiny wood is stained black and carved with a tableau of images that are drawn straight from myth. It sets the tone of any meeting conducted in this room, but I could give a fuck. I'm not here to beg on my knees for a favor. I never have.

Favors from Hades have a way of coming around to bite a person in the ass. I've seen it too many times to discount the danger he represents.

Meg pushes open the doors and they swing easily beneath her fingertips. We precede her into the office. It's done in shades of gray, which would amuse me under other circumstances because I'd bet my left arm that there are fifty of them contained in this room. The far wall is lined with shelves that are filled with knickknacks and weird cluttery shit. I can feel Jasmine's curiosity over the space, but I only have eyes for the man behind the large gray desk.

Hades looks exactly the same as he did last night, though the suit is a little different. He smiles as we walk forward, the smile widening when Meg comes to stand at his right shoulder. "What can I do for you two lovebirds? Need a favor?"

Jasmine tenses, but I don't look at her. "No favors today."

"Pity. We're under quota."

I'm not entirely sure that he's joking, but I ignore it. "You let Ali Tahan have a membership here."

Hades raises his brows. With his black-framed glasses, it gives him the look of a cultured professor waiting for a student to get to the point. "I allow a lot of people to have memberships here. That's the purpose of The Underworld. Neutral territory." His lips quirk, even as his dark eyes stay cold. "Surely you didn't think your vendetta was the exception to the rule?"

I've never seen Ali here, so I made some assumptions I couldn't afford to make. That doesn't change the fact that what happened earlier shouldn't have. "He entered our room without permission and accosted Jasmine."

The amusement on Hades's face vanishes. "Bold accusation."

I give him the look that statement deserves. "You have cameras all over this place. Look for yourself."

Hades glances at Meg. "Be a darling and see what Ali was up to while he was here last night." He watches her leave through the door on the other side of the room, his gaze dropping to her ass.

I almost roll my eyes, but manage to muscle down the reaction. Hades and Meg fuck other people, but the only loyalty they seem to hold is to each other. When it comes to the shit that matters, they are a unified front. I've never actually seen them play together in public, but if they aren't fucking behind closed doors, I'll be shocked.

"Sit, sit. You don't have to stand there all formally." He waves a languid hand to the chairs situated on either side of us. I take the left one and pull Jasmine down into my lap. She tenses for half a second and then relaxes into me. I wish I could say that I'm doing this to send a clear message to Hades, but the truth is that I know she's still shaken and I don't want her to feel untethered.

And, fuck, yes, I want to mark her as mine in front of the king of this place. She doesn't wear my collar, but that's a mere formality at this point.

Hades lifts his brows again, but before he can say something sure to piss me off, Meg walks back into the room. A short nod from her and he turns back to us, all seriousness. "My apologies. We have rules and Ali didn't follow them. It won't happen again. His membership will be rescinded."

And no doubt Hades would take payment for the infraction.

"Thank you." I urge Jasmine to her feet and stand. "See you around, Hades."

"No doubt you will."

I don't hustle Jasmine out of The Underworld, but I set a pace that doesn't invite lingering. Even with Hades's assurances that it won't happen again, I want to get her home.

Safe.

CHAPTER 14

JASMINE

*J*afar doesn't stop touching me the entire ride back to his penthouse. It's not sexual in nature, which I can't decide if I find a relief or a disappointment. Sex would drive away my concern over the interaction with Ali, over the threat he offers that no one saw fit to tell me about until an hour ago, but it won't fix things. I'm rapidly coming to the conclusion that *nothing* will fix my current situation.

He offered to give me my trust.

I might laugh if the gesture didn't make me want to cry. Whether Jafar did it to be cruel or because he honestly thought I'd be able to take it really doesn't matter. Growing up, I had dreams. Dreams of traveling, of moving through the world and experiencing all the things denied me while I remained under my father's thumb. Of carving out a space that was mine and mine alone.

All it took was one night out to lock me up and send panic fluttering in my throat. How can I face the entire world if I can't handle a single club?

Jafar takes my hand and ushers me out of the car. It's not until we leave the elevator into his penthouse that he pulls me to a stop. "Jasmine … Baby girl … Let me take care of you for a little bit."

Take care of me.

I know he doesn't mean it the same way an owner takes care of a pet, but I'm so raw, I can't differentiate between the two truths. If I was stronger, I'd tell him to fuck off and find my balance on my own without needing to lean on another person.

I'm not stronger.

I nod slowly. "Okay."

Jafar doesn't hesitate. He lifts me into his arms. He always seems to be carrying me, and another time I'll have to lay down some ground rules about that, but right now I simply don't have it in me. I let him carry me back to his room and pull the borrowed clothes from my body. He undresses to the waist but no lower, setting the tone for this interaction. No fucking, then.

Again, that flicker between relief and disappointment. I'm so tangled up, I don't know which way I'm supposed to go, how I'm supposed to react.

We end up on the bed, me tucked in his lap with the blankets wrapped around both of us. Jafar's body warms me as much as the blankets do and I finally, finally manage to relax into him.

"There," he murmurs. "I've got you." His big hand smooths down my back and up again, soothing me.

I let my eyes drift shut. Easier to sink into this experience, to let his presence overwhelm my earlier fear. My despair.

Ali is resourceful. I know enough about him to know that. The man didn't get to be where he's at now without having a skillset that lends itself to ill deeds. He can frame his

KATEE ROBERT

narrative as a *rescue* all he wants, conveniently forgetting that he purchased me from my father, but I know the truth.

Not that the truth matters here. It certainly won't stop Ali from trying for me again. "He's not going to stop."

If I'm looking for comforting lies, I'm looking in the wrong place. He sighs. "I know. I have men looking for him right now. It's not enough, though. I'm going to take up the search personally."

"No one could have expected him to accomplish this." I don't know why I'm defending these faceless men of his. If they'd done their job, Ali would be … What would he be? Dead? Can I really condone murder?

I think back to way he looked at me this morning, to the way he always seemed to look at me. Yes, I can condone murder. Better him dead than me forced to live within his control.

I don't know why it's different with Jafar. As displeased as I am with the way he's thrust me into these four walls and restricted my ability to move about, there is now real evidence that I'm not ready for more. I hate that weakness, hate how it hamstrings me when I need to be able to run the most. "Promise me that I can leave when I'm ready."

His hand pauses in the middle of my back. "Elaborate."

"You can't keep me locked up here forever. I'll hate you. I'll *kill* you." My throat tightens, but I force myself to keep speaking, to draw forth this truth into the minuscule space between us. "Don't make the same mistake my father did."

He resumes his slow stroking of my back, but there's a new tension there. "It would be smart to keep you cobbled."

"You would be working on borrowed time." I can't live like this forever. I don't know what the future holds, but if I wanted to be a dangerous man's sex toy, I could have married Ali. The thought of his hands on my body sends a shudder through me.

"We'll talk about this later." He wraps his arms around me and pulls me close. "I recognize that this isn't ideal for you, but until things are under control, I can't risk you being hurt."

If I was a little more idealistic, I'd think he's expressing concern over my welfare because he cares about me. I know better. The state of my person entirely reflects on Jafar's power. It did when he dressed me in his shirt and hauled me out of my father's house over his shoulder. It did when he fingered me in front of the man who holds the territory to the south

And it did when Ali slipped into my room after I was left without protection.

Business. That's all I am to Jafar. And a warm woman to sink his cock into and play his games. A symbol of his might.

I push against his chest. "I'd like to sleep now."

"Baby girl." He captures my chin and lifts my face. His brows are drawn and he doesn't look particularly happy at my attempt to create distance. "What's going through that head of yours?"

"Nothing but the truth."

"Tell me."

Anger blossoms in me, a fragile flower I cultivate as if my life depends on it. My life may not, but my heart does. I let it bleed into my eyes, let him see exactly how torn and battered I feel. "You have access to everything I am. Allow me a private thought from time to time."

There's something on his face, a flicker of indecision, as if I've surprised him and he doesn't know the best way to play this. It's all a game, after all. Jafar may have mentioned marriage, but if he strong-arms me into going through with it, it will be in name only. I almost smile wryly. Well, I don't imagine we'll stop fucking, but there will be no love there. No equality.

I deserve better.

"Let me go."

"Baby girl," he says again, and this time he sounds just as tired as I feel. "Haven't you learned by now? Every part of you belongs to me. Your body, your brain, your heart. All mine."

This time, when I push away from him, he allows it. The fact that he *allows* it, that I can't do even this on my own, it's too much. I fight my way off the giant bed and stand on shaking legs. "I don't belong to you."

"Yes, you do."

I turn around and walk away. I have to. If I don't establish some kind of distance, the *smallest* kind of distance, right now, then I'm lost forever.

All I want to do is crawl back into that bed and let him tell me that everything will be okay. That he really does care. That no matter how unconventional the beginning of this relationship was, it *is* a relationship. I want him to tell me a lot of things.

No, not things.

Lies.

And because they're lies, because he might just deliver them as if they're the god's honest truth, I have to walk away.

His voice stops me when I reach the door, the snap of command stilling my feet despite myself. "Jasmine." I don't turn, don't answer. I simply wait. Thankfully, he doesn't make me wait long. "I meant what I said—I'm going after Ali. I might not be home for a few days, but you'll be safe here."

I press my lips together, hating how worried I am about him. "Okay."

"Tink will be here Monday morning."

He scheduled the appointment with her that I asked for. "Thank you, Daddy." My lips form the words without thinking, and I can't even manage to make it sarcastic.

"It's a mutual addiction." A pause, and then his voice lashes me. "Can't have you aching and empty, can we? If I'm not there to fill you up, you'll have to make do with your fingers."

I eagerly skate a hand down the center of my body to push two fingers as deep as I can. I must make a sound, something desperate and needy, because he doesn't hesitate to keep talking, spinning his web of lust tighter around me. "You're a wicked girl, aren't you? How many times did you play with that pretty pussy and think about me while you were in your father's house?"

A small voice tells me to lie, but I'm too far gone already. "A lot."

"A lot," he repeats slowly. As if it's new knowledge. As if we didn't spend so much of last night reenacting fantasies that we both had during the last five years.

I shouldn't tell him more, shouldn't reveal yet another fault line for him to take advantage of. And yet I can't seem to help it. "Every time we verbally sparred, I'd go upstairs and touch myself. Every time, I'd be just like I am right now. Wet. Aching."

His low curse is so incredibly vindicating. Each time his facade cracks, just a little, he reminds me that I'm not the only one lost at sea with this arrangement. I fuck myself slowly with my fingers, relishing the tease, the way pleasure builds in slow waves. I cup one breast and pluck at my nipple, the light pain causing desire to spike higher, to bring me closer to the edge.

"Your birthday last year." He still sounds hoarse with need, but the command is back in his voice. "You wore that little cocktease of a red dress. You stopped in the hallway to fix your shoe."

Heat suffuses me. "I knew you were there." I'd bent at the waist intentionally, feeling just as wicked and dirty as I do right now. I hadn't known then what I wanted to accomplish, had only aimed to make him miss a step.

"It took everything I had not to touch you then. To walk up and drag those lacy black panties to the side and tongue you right there in the hallway."

I can picture it exactly as he describes. The party was going on in the next room, loud and boisterous like all the parties in that house were. I can feel Jafar behind me, the rough touch as he yanks my panties to the side, his breath on my pussy. I withdraw my fingers to circle my clit. It's nowhere near as good as his mouth, but it builds the fantasy around me the same way his voice does. "I could come from that. Right there."

"Better be quiet. If someone walks in …" Another low curse and I know without a shadow a doubt that he's got his cock in his hand and he's jerking himself. "You taste too good to stop, baby girl. A man could lose himself in the way you try to fight down those moans of pleasure, in the way you writhe against my tongue. I need to have you coming all over my face."

"I'll be quiet. I promise," I whisper, still circling my clit. There's not enough air in the room. My whole body tightens in anticipation and I slow my touch, needing to draw it out. "I'll spread my legs for you. Let you in."

"Good girl." His breathing is just as ragged as mine now. "We're running out of time. Every second—do you hear someone walking our way?"

I can almost feel the heavy footsteps coming down the hall. It's too much. I press hard on my clit and cry out as I come. Distantly, I can hear him saying my name, the syllables gone hoarse as he follows me over the edge. I lay there in my bed and stare at the ceiling. Difficult to remember that I'm still furious with him, with the situation, with my entire life.

No doubt that's the point, but I can't dredge up the energy to be irritated by it. "Thank you."

"Believe me when I say it's my pleasure." Now, I *know* I hear the amusement in his voice. "Enjoy the rest of your day."

CHAPTER 15

JASMINE

I spend the weekend in a strange sort of haze. I swim, I watch movies, I do my best to entertain myself until I pass out exhausted in my bed.

Every night, Jafar comes to me. He wakes me with a touch, a hand stroking down my spine or through my hair. In the dark of my room, he explores my body with his hands and then his mouth, our respective silences making the entire experience feel like a fever dream. It doesn't matter if I'm riding his cock or if he's driving me deeper into the mattress with the force of his thrusts. It's so surreal, I can almost convince myself I hallucinate the experiences.

Every morning, I wake to find him gone except for a note beside my bed.

By Monday, I'm going out of my fucking mind. I want to *see* him, to go another round of verbally sparring, to do something other than wait and try not to think too hard about the danger Jafar is in by hunting Ali.

I'm desperate for the distraction Tink represents, and so I'm impatiently waiting for her when she walks through the elevator doors. Today she's dressed in a pair of flirty floral culottes that kick out with every step and a white lace top that only seems emphasized by the bra I can see through it. She gives me a look that's almost an apology, and it's the only warning I have before a second woman pushes another rack of clothing into the penthouse.

Even in everyday clothing, I'd recognize Meg anywhere. She wears a black jumpsuit that dips low between her breasts, offering a flash of pale skin that is all the more tantalizing because it's the only thing remotely scandalous about her outfit. She offers me a slow smile. "I hope you don't mind my crashing the party."

Tink snorts and sets to work getting the racks arranged how she wants them. "As if we have a choice. You're the boss lady."

"Hardly." Meg lifts one shoulder in a graceful shrug. "We all answer to Hades."

She seemed happy enough to stand at his right hand the other night, but if I've learned anything, it's that appearances can be deceiving. It's a whole new world out there, and I can't afford to assume anything. "Good afternoon, Meg."

"So proper, this one." She shares a telling glance with Tink. "We're not on the books right now. You can relax."

Somehow, I don't think that's remotely the truth. I wonder if Jafar knows Meg planned on showing up when he's not around, and I suspect he wouldn't like it. I open my mouth to tell her as much, but stop myself. We're in Jafar's penthouse, and no doubt the exits are all watched by guards and more cameras than I care to think about. It's not as if Meg can knock me over the head and smuggle me off to a secondary location.

I finally perch on the edge of the couch across the one she's sprawled over. "You have a reason for being here."

"Do I?" She stops playing with her hair and gives me a slow grin that sends my stomach tumbling over itself.

"Maybe I just wanted to play, Jasmine. You're a gorgeous girl, and watching Jafar fuck you was really something else."

My skin heats at the thought of what kind of games she could mean, but it's a distant feeling. Not overwhelming like my desire for Jafar. I am attracted to Meg. If Jafar arranged for us to play in the kind of scenario he described the other night, I would allow myself to be swept away.

But not like this.

Not behind his back.

I keep my spine straight and my expression even. "Tell me why you're really here or get out."

She considers me for a long moment and shrugs. Just like that, all signs of seduction disappear and she goes cold in a way that has me realizing exactly how badly I've underestimated her. Meg leans forward and props her elbows on her knees. "I can get you out."

I barely dare draw breath. I don't let myself look to where Tink stands to the side, uncharacteristically silent. "Excuse me?"

"You're a pretty bird locked in a prettier cage." She flicks a hand to encompass the penthouse. "I can get you out."

"Freedom doesn't feel much like freedom when I have nothing." Jafar offered to release my trust fund. I don't know that I trust him enough to believe that it's not some kind of trap, but I certainly don't trust *Meg* to offer something without a thousand strings attached.

She eyes me. "I'll give you enough funds to get you going and a new identity that can pave the way for a fresh start. You show every evidence of being a smart girl. I'm sure you'll land on your feet if you give yourself the chance to."

Temptation slithers through me. She's the snake in the garden of Eden, whispering about a world I've only glimpsed through the wall that surrounds me. Offering me freedom that might be anything but. "There's a catch."

"The only catch is that you leave Carver City and don't come back. I can cover your trail so no one will find you as long as you're not an idiot."

Her plan unfurls before me, and I can almost admire her for the move. Without me here, playing the part of the war prize, Jafar's position will be weakened. I doubt it's enough to oust him completely, but it means that he'll be challenged. Repeatedly. It will keep him busy enough that he won't be able to look to expand until he's ground up every bit of rebellion within his own territory. I tilt my head to the side. "You have no reason to think Jafar won't be happy with what he has."

"Smart little thing, aren't you?" A little respect filters into her blue eyes. "Jafar was born hungry. He might be satisfied with what he has for a few years, but eventually he'll start eyeing the territory boundaries and pushing against the other players. He'll take Hook first, because it's the smallest amount of ground to cover, but that will only buoy him." She shakes her head. "We don't exactly have peace in Carver City, but what we have is close enough to it. No one is allowed to rock the boat. Not even Jafar."

On the surface, it makes sense, but ...

Something's still off.

"What price?"

Meg doesn't blink. "What price can you put on freedom? No, Jasmine. No price, no deal. Just an offer that's mutually beneficial."

I don't know if I believe her. Does it make sense to undermine Jafar now, rather than wait until he's secured his base? Yes, most definitely. But after Tink's talk about Hades's deals —and this offer can only come from Hades, for all that it's Meg's mouth forming the words—I can't help thinking that there's another shoe waiting to drop. That when it does, it will crush me.

Either way, I'd be a fool to turn her down completely. "Can I think about it?"

"Sure." Another of those graceful shrugs. "But the offer expires in seven days, so think fast." She pushes to her feet and smiles. "See you around, Jasmine."

I don't move until the elevator doors close behind her, and even then I count to ten slowly before I let the steel bleed out of my spine and slump back against the couch. "Is it always like that with her?"

Tink snorts. "Usually, it's worse." She gives herself a shake. "Rumor has it that Meg was like you when she first got to Carver City. A princess, for all intents and purposes, though she left everything to flee ... I don't know. Something. It'd have to be bad to rattle *her*." She flips through the racks and tosses me a dress. "She found her way to Hades and made a deal."

I drop my robe and pull on the dress. It's a style actually suitable for day wear, a sheath dress in a cream that looks good with my darker coloring. "What kind of deal?"

"Dunno. Hades doesn't exactly proclaim the terms from the top of the tallest tower." She eyes me. "That's a keeper. Try this one."

Another dress, this one a deep red that's fitted through the torso and flares out around my hips, the hem stopping just past my knees. "I like it."

"Of course you do. I picked it for you." She waits for me to strip out of it and sets it aside in the pile. "But anyway, that was before my time. As long as I've been around, it's Meg and Hades, Hades and Meg."

I give myself a few moments to indulge in the fantasy of being the right hand to a man like that. To Jafar. Meg and Hades are as close to equals as I've ever seen. Maybe they even *are* equals, their relationship originating in a deal or no.

Jafar and I will never get there. He's too intent on keeping me closed in, keeping me safe, simply keeping me. "There's something romantic about that."

"If you say so." She shrugs and passes over another garment. "I'm not going to tell you not to take her offer, but, be careful, princess. Meg can be cool, but she's as much about the bottom line as Hades. A deal is a mess, but at least they'll honor their part of it. Once Hades gives his word, it's as good as done. This offer stinks."

I'm inclined to agree, but having an escape hatch is attractive in a way I can't put into words. This is the first time in my life I've had actual options, albeit ones that aren't overly attractive. I can stay with Jafar, continue to be his ... I'm not even sure what I am to him.

Prize. Statement. Submissive.

He's not a complete sociopath, so he treats me well enough, but that could very well be linked to wanting to keep me docile so I'll keep fucking him. I press my fingertips to my temples. "This whole thing hurts my head."

"I don't envy you. My deal is shit, but at least it's straightforward."

I open my mouth to ask what her deal is, but reconsider at last moment. If she wants me to know, she'll tell me. "What would you do?"

"Can't tell you that." Tink pulls out a dress, looks at it, and puts it back on the rack. "You have to make the choice you can live with, whatever that looks like."

She's right. It's a choice I have to make for myself, for better or worse. I manage a smile. "I appreciate you being frank with me."

"You don't have a lot of allies. I'm a dick, but even I can't kick someone when they're down." She turns with two pairs of pants in her hands. "Now, onto more important things. Jeans or slacks? What are you feeling?"

"Jeans." I've only owned a single pair and I had to sneak

them in because my father had strong opinions about what was considered appropriate clothing. Denim didn't make the cut.

"Girl after my own heart." She pulls out several more pairs and drops them next to me. "Work through this pile and tell me what you like and we'll go from there."

We pass the next hour like that, and I can tell Tink intentionally keeps the conversation away from trickier topics. As much as I want to drill her for information, I allow it. She's been kind to me, but at the end of the day, she owes her allegiance to Hades and I'm not fool enough to think two styling appointments can sway that.

After she leaves, I dress carefully. I don't know what Jafar has planned for tonight, and even as part of me tangles with the concept of taking Meg's offer, the rest of me is abuzz with anticipation.

How can this be?

The only thing I've ever wanted is to be free. To make my own choices, to live without a sword hanging over my neck. To move through the world as a normal person.

Meg's offer would give me that.

No doubt I'd have to make some allowances for lifestyle. She may give me enough money to get me started, but I'll have to learn fast on my feet, starting from the ground up. The idea of it is staggering. Just a few nights ago, I told Jafar I couldn't do it on my own. What if I was wrong? What if I *can*?

He won't let me go.

Even if he releases my trust fund—and I have my doubts about that—he won't let me leave the city. I can pretend having money of my own will put us closer to equal footing, but it's a lie. Jafar is too overwhelming. He touches me, and I forget all the reasons I don't want any of the life he's shoved me into. I start to think that maybe this beautiful cage isn't so bad, as long as he's in here with me.

Except he's *not* in here with me.

He has all the power.

I have none.

Jafar walks out of the elevators as I pour a glass of wine. He looks a decadent as ever, though the image is smudged. His charcoal suit is tailored to perfection, but his brown skin glistens as if he's recently run. The thought of Jafar running home to me is too intoxicating to dwell on, so I turn my attention to his hair. He's due for a cut; the waves have morphed into curls, a change that almost makes him seem more approachable.

More touchable.

He checks his stride and pivots to head in my direction, his purposeful steps eating up the length of the living room. He rounds the kitchen island and stops short. I try not to warm at the way he drinks in the sight of me, but it's a heady feeling to have Jafar's full attention. To have him *appreciating*.

I take a shaky sip of my wine. "You're late."

"I'm sorry." The apology might sound more sincere if his voice hadn't dropped an octave. "There was a complication."

I don't want to ask, but I can't seem to help myself. "Ali?"

"Still in the wind." Jafar nods at the wine bottle. "Pour me one?"

If he tried to command me, I might dig in my heels simply for the sake of doing it. I've already lost so much, and every moment I spend in his presence is a moment where I question whether I really want to escape.

Yes. The answer *must* be yes.

I pour a second glass of wine and pass it over. Jafar takes a long drink and leans a hip against the counter. For the first time in … ever … he looks like a man. Simply a man. Gorgeous beyond belief, yes, but merely human instead of this hurricane that rips me from my foundations with every word and touch.

He runs a hand through his hair, the move obviously the source of his curls getting the best of him. "I underestimated him."

I blink. "You mean you're not all-knowing and all-powerful?"

"Very funny, brat." His second drink of wine is shorter, but the tension riding his shoulders seems to ease a little. "The majority of my focus was on undermining your father and staging the coup. If I had waited, this wouldn't be an issue, because I could have handled them both at the same time. But, I didn't wait." A shrug. "I'll get him in the end. He's good, but I'm better."

I pick apart that statement. He's said something to the same effect before, but we usually end up fighting or fucking before I can dig deeper. "You changed your timeline for me."

For a moment, I think he might deflect. "Yes. I could tell you that the reason is because a marriage is a whole hell of a lot harder to dismantle than a parental relationship when it comes to a shift of power, and it'd even be the truth. But not the full truth." He sets his glass down and meets my gaze directly. "I've seen what's left of the women who share Ali's bed."

My breath stalls in my lungs. I reach for a response, *any* response, to dispel the tension building between us. I try for a wry smile. "Does he chase them through his house and then fuck them right there in the middle of the floor when he catches them?"

"Don't do that." Jafar shakes his head.

"Don't do what?" I'm being intentionally dense, but we're posed on the edge of precipice and I don't know what will happen to us if we tumble over the edge. We won't be able to go back. That's the only certainty.

He doesn't move from his spot, doesn't approach to touch me in a way that will bring me to my knees in submission. His brows draw down over dark eyes. "Have I ever done anything to do you that you didn't want?"

I expect a challenge in the question, a prideful assertion of a truth we both know. Of course he's never done anything to me that I didn't want. I've desired Jafar ever since I set eyes on him, first because he was forbidden to me and, later, because I like the way I spark to life when he's near. Our verbal sparring sessions were the highlight of my life, a few short minutes where I felt like a real person and not simply a golem, going through the motions at someone else's command.

Except that's not what I see in his expression.

He looks almost sick.

"I've wanted it. All of it. More." Words to damn me. Words to pass him all the power and leave me quivering at his feet. How am I supposed to walk away from this man when his key turns my lock in a way I've only ever read about? If my books are to be believed, this kind of connection comes around once in a lifetime, if you're lucky. What kind of fool would I be to run from that?

One who wants to be free.

Jafar nods slowly. "To the original topic—I couldn't let him get his hands on you, so I moved the timeline."

I'm not naive enough to think that he did it solely for me. He's told me as much. It doesn't change the fact that my safety has never been a priority for anyone. Oh, the safety of my body to keep my father's prized possession in peak condition and unmarred? Yes, that mattered. But that's not what Jafar is talking about. Not bruises and cuts and things that will heal given enough time.

He's talking about wounds that will scar even if no one can see evidence of them on my skin.

I sip my wine. "Thank you?"

"Don't thank me. If I had half a conscience, I wouldn't have taken you."

And then Ali would have tracked me down and brought me back. That's the truth, one we've discussed between us. I don't understand why he's conveniently forgetting it now, why he's chosen to flog himself with our situation. I frown. "What happened this weekend?" This is the moment, the precipice, the point of no return where he'll let me in or he'll keep me walled up in this penthouse in the name of safety. I hold my breath and wait.

Jafar picks up his wine glass again. "Have you thought about starting school?"

It takes every skill I possess to keep my expression placid despite the dizzying feeling of being dashed to pieces. Jafar cares about me. Even if he's a cold bastard, I've never really doubted that. But he doesn't see me as capable, not really. I'm a valued possession, a pet who needs careful care taking in order to thrive. I'm not strong enough to be equal to him.

If I stay here, I never will be.

CHAPTER 16

JAFAR

*S*omething's changed, and I can't put my finger on what. It doesn't help that I'm distracted over this clusterfuck of a weekend. Six of my men are gone, disappeared as if they never existed, and I have only Ali to blame. He's not scared of the force I can bring against him, and he's not in the wind like I first thought. If anything, getting access to Jasmine at The Underworld emboldened him. He'll keep striking until I put him down, but I can't fucking *find* him to remove the threat he represents.

When Jasmine doesn't answer, I prod her again. "School?"

"Oh." She examines her wine glass. "I suppose I'd like to college, but I haven't put much thought into it."

She's not telling me the truth. I can see it in the way her eyes drop, in the nervous twitch of her fingers against the counter. She told no lies when she said she's wanted everything I've given her and more, but she's lying now.

"I find that hard to believe." I keep my voice mild. "The entire time I've known you, you've had your face pressed against the bars of your cage and your eyes on the future. Don't tell me that plan didn't include college."

Jasmine gives me a brittle smile. "When would I have gone to college, Jafar? When I married some man like Ali? Future plans aren't for people like me. I'm a pawn in a larger game. I always have been."

Who is this woman? Where is the fire that seems ready to burst from her skin normally? I lean back and cross my arms over my chest. "You're going to college."

The look she gives me can only be described as withering. "That's not your decision to make."

"I think you'll find that it is." I don't know why she's resisting, but it doesn't make a difference. No matter what Jasmine thinks of me, I have no plans to keep her walled up in this tower indefinitely. It's not reasonable. Beyond that, it makes me look weak as fuck to have to lock my woman away in order to protect her. She might not see herself as mine, but everyone else does.

I do.

Life would be easier if that was my only motivation. Bolstering strength and keeping up appearances. That shit I understand. It's not, though. I want Jasmine to find her feet in a real way. She's never had a chance before, and I can be the one to give it to her. Is there a whole lot of possessive pride wrapped up in that sentiment? Yes. I won't deny it. I want her to fly and to know I was the one who gave her that chance.

I want her to choose me.

The thought almost makes me laugh. Since when did I get so goddamn sentimental? "Tell me something, baby girl."

"What do you want to know?" She sounds so cold, so prim, I want to make a mess of her.

"Are you digging in your heels simply for the sake of doing it? Because you're wasting both our time."

She finally looks at me, *really* looks at me. There are shadows in her dark eyes that I have no solution to. I am not a caretaker, not a gentle soul that will love her into healing. I wouldn't know the first place to start with that shit. I have the skills I've cultivated over my life, and those will have to be good enough. I push off the counter and hold out a hand. "Come on."

"What?"

"I think this is a conversation better had under different circumstances." I wait for her to take my hand and then I haul her over my shoulder. She curses and smacks my back, but I like carrying Jasmine. It soothes something raw inside me to know she's fully mine, even if only for the duration of the trip. I take the elevator down a floor and stride to the little set-up I ordered put together when I realized Ali had slipped through my grasp again. There will be a time where I'll happily go out on the town with Jasmine on my arm, but it's too dangerous right now. Ali is a loose cannon, and while I don't think he'd snipe Jasmine—not yet—he's riling up others who might not have the same restraint.

Not to mention the man won't react well when he realizes that he'll never lay a hand on Jasmine. Not again.

I set her down slowly, letting her body drag along mine. She presses her hands to my chest and glares up at me. "You have to realize that you can't just lug me around whenever you feel like it."

"Do I?" I shouldn't enjoy needling her this much, but she's finally snapping and flickering at me, exhibiting the fire I know she carries deep inside. I want it closer to the surface. I don't want her control.

I just want Jasmine.

Fuck, but I'm in trouble. She was only ever meant to be the pawn she describes herself as, except I'm self-aware enough to acknowledge the truth. This woman worked her way beneath my skin a long time ago. Now that I've had her in my home, that I've seen her wild with abandon and

159

desire, now that I know exactly how hard she gets off on being bad?

I've always dealt in cold hard facts. Ambition like mine can get a man killed if he's not careful, and I worked my way up the ranks using my brain instead of letting emotion get the best of me. That trait is what makes me better than anyone else around me, and it's the reason Balthazar never saw me coming. For all his power, he was ruled by impulse and anger and, beneath that, fear.

But if I was the type of man to give way to fantasy, to dream up a woman to be my match in every way?

I don't have to look far to find her.

She's standing right in front of me.

I sure as fuck don't know how to feel about that. Wanting something—some*one*—this badly is like handing my enemies a loaded gun and relying on a prayer to some imaginary god to save me. They'll see her as my weak point and they'll come for her. They'll *keep* coming for her.

"Jafar?" She slides her hands up my chest, her brows furrowed. "Daddy, are you okay? You're shaking."

I lock it down. I don't have another choice. Confessing any of this shit to her is out of the question. She's still got her eye on the door, and knowing that she'll rip me apart if she tries to leave won't be enough to stop her. I'd be a fucking idiot to believe otherwise. "Eat with me."

She blinked those big, dark eyes at me. "I don't understand you."

"You don't have to understand to play along."

No smile in response. Just a searching look. "Is that all this is? A game to play?"

I can't dredge up a lie. "No, baby girl. That's not all this is."

She parts her lips like she wants to pepper me with more questions, but she finally shakes her head and turns to look at the hastily put together set up in the room. It doesn't *look* last minute, of course. My people are better than that. A small round table sits in the center of the room with two tall candles and a full array of silverware and plates. If I can't take her out for the night I had planned, I'll bring it to her.

Finally, Jasmine looks back at me. "Okay, I'll put aside my feelings for the night if that's what you want."

I don't want her to put aside her feelings. I want to shift the feelings themselves. I can't tell her that. She might grab one of the butter knives and try to stab me with it. The thought brings a smile. "Do you often attempt to stab people?"

She moves to the table and I follow to pull out her chair. Jasmine doesn't answer until she's seated. "Only when they sneak into my room in the middle of the night."

I can still feel the prick of the blade against my groin. She'd stood a good chance of hitting an artery and leaving me to bleed out on her bedroom floor. And, sick bastard that I am, all I felt was a sense of pride. "If I'd been Ali, would you have followed through on the threat?"

"Yes." She takes her napkin and spreads it across her lap. "I assumed that anyone in my room uninvited was up to no good." She arches an eyebrow at me. "I was correct."

I chuckle. "Yes, you were." I lean back as a trio of my men come in, all carrying covered plates. We don't speak as they set them on the table, remove the covers, and silently leave the room. I watch Jasmine take in the food. "This looks like paella from Rom's."

"It is."

Surprise flares, quickly banked. "You know my favorite place."

"I think we've established that my fascination with you has prodded me to learn all number of things."

She picks up her fork and considers me. "You say fascina-tion, but if I wasn't attracted to you, it would border on terrifying." Another long look at her plate. "I'm not sure it *doesn't* border on terrifying."

"Eat before it gets cold."

She gives me another of those saucy looks I've come to crave and we dig in. She's correct that this food comes from Rom, who runs a restaurant that I'm reasonably sure has no name, but I'm not about to tell her that I paid the man an exorbitant amount of money to cook for us personally tonight. She'll accuse me of padding her cage with pleasant experiences, and it's exactly what I'm doing. I know she's restless, but I can't do a damn thing about it until Ali is removed. Even then, I can't allow her free rein. Not until I can guarantee her safety.

It's only when she sets her fork aside that I resume our earlier conversation. "Why did you lie to me about college?"

Jasmine sighs. "Do you ever get tired of moving me around the board on your whim? Princess in a palace. Princess in a penthouse. Submissive in The Underworld. Now college co-ed? Why do you insist on pushing me like this?"

I should feed her a line, but I find myself answering honestly. "You've been walled up for too long."

"I've been walled up too long," she repeats, as if she can't have heard me right. Jasmine picks up her wine glass, seems to reconsider, and sets it down again. "You are such a hypocrite."

"Guilty."

My easy admission seems to set her back. She glares. "I lied about college because I know what comes from playing my hand too openly. You already have all the power and I have none. I'm not going to simply gift you with every piece of me."

"Too bad. That's exactly what I want."

She shakes her head. "No."

We'll get there. I have plenty of time to play the long game with this. I ease back. "Tell me about college."

"Fine." She smooths her dress and meets my gaze. "I want to major in software engineering."

Now it's my turn to blink in surprise. "I didn't see that coming."

"Why would you? All you see is a pretty face. All *anyone* sees is a pretty face. No one bothers to ask me what I want, or what my interests are. They certainly don't stop to think that my brain might be more valuable to the business than my pussy is."

I'm guilty of that, but I'm not about to apologize. I saw more of her than either her father or Ali did, but apparently I didn't see deeply enough. "Talk me through it."

She considers me, probably expecting me to laugh at her expense, but I genuinely want to hear her thoughts on it. I've underestimated Jasmine again and again, and I'm determined to course-correct. Finally, she draws herself up. "Many of our day-to-day operations are borderline archaic. Creating counterfeit paper money?" She shakes her head. "It's time to step into the future. A large percentage of the world's wealth is digital now. With the right minds involved, we could take a stake in that with half the manpower and significantly less overhead cost."

"Paper money works." It's also one of the least offensive things we do in our territory.

"Yes, yes." She waves that away. "I wouldn't dream of decreasing that operation. My point is that balance is key. Relying only on paper money is like nibbling at crumbs that have fallen from a table piled high with food. We can increase our profit exponentially if we do it correctly."

We.

I don't think she realizes what she's said, the slip of her tongue that indicates the truth—when she looks into the future, she sees us there together. I choose not to comment on it, enjoying this conversation too much to push her on a personal front. "How many people would you need?"

Her smile fades slowly. "I don't know. The college degree was only the start of it, and I'm already seven years behind where I would be if my father had allowed it when I first suggested the idea. I stopped looking into programs when he cut off that option. I wouldn't even know where to start."

My offer to send her to college was as much to keep her busy as to help her blossom. This is something else altogether. "Have you considered a less traditional education?"

"Jafar, I haven't considered *anything* until an hour ago when you sprang this on me. After my father forbade me from going to college, I managed to learn the basics on my own, but it seemed too cruel to continue when it wouldn't amount to anything."

I incline my head to acknowledge her point, but I'm already spinning out possibilities. "It shouldn't be too difficult to find someone with the skillset you're talking about. They'd have to come here, of course, but we can arrange that." I tap my fingers on the table. "I'll get Jeremiah looking into it tomorrow." I could ask Hades. He has the kind of connections that ensure he can find anything or anyone, so a person with this skillset should be child's play. But there is the price of his help to consider. I won't ask him until I'm sure I can't do it myself.

"Just like that."

"Just like that."

She gives me a look like she's never seen me before. "I don't understand you. You lock me up but then you do this. And there's the sex."

Amusement flickers through me, but I push it down deep. She might give the impression of a kitten staring at a grasshopper, but I know better. The woman has claws. I won't undermine her wavering self-confidence, and once I decide that, it's the easiest thing in the world to relax into this conversation. "Elaborate."

"I'm sorry, I was assuming you could pull the thought right out of my mind the same way you do with my sexual fantasies."

Ah. That.

I take a long drink of my wine and consider her. "We've spent a long time circling each other, baby girl. Over the years, you've given yourself away in a thousand different tells, but the real deciding factor was the night I staged the coup." My blood heats at the memory. "I would have let you walk out, you know."

"I know." She fiddles with her napkin. "I wanted you to catch me."

"I'm aware."

She frowns. "You've checked in with me a lot, haven't you? Not overtly, but you're constantly analyzing and shifting to accommodate my reactions." Jasmine frowns harder. "It's hard to tell in the moment, but that's the truth, isn't it?"

"Yes." I set my wine glass down. "No matter what flavor of games we play, it's about giving you what you need."

"And what do *you* need."

"You." The admission slips free before I can stop it. Too late to take it back, to alter the course I've just set us on.

"Jafar," She looks away. "How can this ever work?"

I reach across the table and take her hand. The touch does little to steady me. There's no convenient map of our path forward. Jasmine might trust me with her body, but she doesn't trust me with her heart. If I was a better man, I'd respect that. I wouldn't push her. I'd seduce her slowly until I'm the only one she can imagine herself with.

I don't know how to do that shit. I can play cultured with

the best of them, but the man that emerges whenever I get my hands on her is the true me. Rough. Possessive. Unexpectedly tender at times. I can't force her to trust me, so I'll have to wait her out. It's the only option. I stand and tug her to her feet. "It will work because it's us."

"I truly wish I could believe that."

"You don't have to believe it, baby girl. I'll believe enough for both of us."

CHAPTER 17

JASMINE

*I*t would be the easiest thing in the world to fall in love with Jafar.

As the remains of our dinner are taken away, leaving us staring over the table at each other, I'm forced to admit the truth—I'm more than halfway there. I wish I could find joy in that knowledge. Love is supposed to be this wonderful, all-encompassing feeling that sends flowers springing to life inside me and has me walking around with a foolish grin on my face. This doesn't feel anything like that.

It feels like being in the middle of a violent storm, and Jafar is the only thing anchoring me in place. Everything *hurts*. If butterflies ever existed in my stomach, they've been replaced by something with claws and teeth.

These violent delights have violent ends.

Romeo and Juliet is not a romantic arc I wish to mirror, throwing away everything for a man. At least Juliet had *something* before love swept her away. My family, what little of it there was, has been murdered. Any power I possess is all illusion. Enemies lurk in the shadows.

If I was a smarter woman, I would number Jafar among them.

"I have something special planned for you tonight."

His low words coax me from my dark thoughts, and I'm only too happy to let his sheer presence wash away my concerns. At least for a little while. Tomorrow is soon enough to worry about the future, about the implications of what Jafar has laid out tonight.

He wants to keep me happy.

That should be a positive. I want to *be* happy. But my needs and his are forever at odds. He wants me content in this place. I need to be free.

Tomorrow. I'll form a plan tomorrow.

I finally dredge up a smile for him. "Something special?"

"Yes." He takes me hand and pulls me to my feet. I tense, half expecting him to toss me over his shoulder again, but Jafar seems content to tug me along behind him. "Under other circumstances, this would go down at The Underworld, but some adjustments were required."

Because of Ali.

I should be happy Jafar wants to keep me out of that man's hands. I *am* happy about that. It's losing The Underworld as a destination away from the penthouse that I can't stand. My cage keeps closing tighter around me, the trap teeth digging in deeper to my limbs. A constant reminder that I have no control of my life.

Jafar leads me into the lounge, and I stop short. "Meg?"

Meg leans against the bar, a wicked smile painting her lips. "Apparently play time came early." She winks. "You should thank your Daddy for me. I'm truly a gift."

I turn to Jafar. "You ..." He set this up for me, because I expressed interest.

He sinks his hands into my hair and pulls me forward to press against his chest. His dark eyes see everything I can't put into words. "It's my pleasure to meet your needs, baby girl. *All* of them." His glances over my shoulder and I don't know what knowledge has passed between him and Meg, but I can hear her moving behind me. "Working up to the other fantasy starts here."

The other fantasy.

The one where he invites more people. Where we jump from them watching to them taking me up on the invitation simmering in my blood. I open my mouth, but it's as if all the air has disappeared from the room. It takes me three tries to force out the words. "Thank you, Daddy."

He tugs on my hair, forcing my attention to narrow in on him. "It's the same rules. Safe word and it stops."

Which allows me to resist, to fight them, to drive my desire higher every time they overpower me. I lick my lips. "I understand."

"Good."

Just like that, he goes cold, his expression closing down in a way that has my heart leaping into my chest. He releases my hair and grasps my chin. "You've been teasing again, baby girl."

"No," I whisper. I jerk away, and he allows me to take a step before he spins me around and pins me against his chest. Meg's moved to the couch and she has a tumbler of amber colored liquid dangling from one hand and her legs crossed. She's wearing another suit, the gray pants perfectly tailored to her body and the white blouse translucent enough that I can see the faint outline of her nipples through it. Her mass of dark brown hair is pulled back from her face and she's done something with her makeup that emphasizes the wicked slyness in her blue eyes. Dark red lipstick finishes the look and, yes, my entire body goes tight at the realization that she's going to do more than look tonight.

Jafar moves closer to the couch, forcing me in front of

him. "I invite Meg over for a nice drink and you come in here in *that* dress."

"You bought me this dress," I protest, pushing back against him, trying not to roll my ass against his hard cock. Wanton. Every time we play this game, Jafar makes me feel absolutely *wanton*. He boils me down to my very essence, to pure lust, pulling forth fantasy after fantasy and delivering them without qualm. The man is addiction personified.

"I bought you that dress to wear for *me*." He moves us forward another step. "Not so you can flash your pussy at our guests."

Meg takes a sip of her drink, as relaxed as if we're having a normal conversation and Jafar isn't forcing me closer and closer to her in short steps designed to draw out the journey. She tilts her head to the side. "She's got a pretty pussy, Jafar. No wonder she wants to show it off."

"You're wrong," I whisper.

"Am I?" She shrugs as if she doesn't care one way or another. "I think your Daddy is right."

"She likes to play the tease." His dark promise has me struggling in earnest. I dig in my heels and thrash, the movements driving the hem of my dress higher. Jafar pins my wrists at the small of my back and tsks. "Look at her, Meg. Putting on a show even now."

I struggle harder, but he bands his other arm around my waist and lifts me off my feet entirely. Two steps and we're to the couch. I bite my bottom lip. "Stop."

"Jafar." Meg's voice is low, her amusement as cutting as Jafar's threats. "Your hospitality leaves something to be desired if you can't even train your girl correctly."

"We're a work in process." He moves my hands up to either side of his neck. "Keep them there."

"But—"

"If you're going to disobedient, I'll tie you down."

Oh god.

Meg leans forward, which is right around the time I realize she's even with my hips, where my short dress has ridden up to indecent heights. She runs her thumbs along the hem of the dress, inching it a little higher, baring me. "No panties. A liar in addition to a little tease."

"I did tell you." Jafar kicks my feet apart and spears a finger deep inside me. He withdraws before I can do more than gasp and holds it up. Another of those tsks that I love and hate in equal measure. "Meg, she's ten seconds from getting off, all because she's put you in a bad way."

"Wicked girl," Meg murmurs. She looks over my shoulder, and I have no idea what she and Jafar communicate in that look. They have a history, but somehow the very thing that made me jealous a few days ago seems so ... mundane. Something left over from the world of *shouldn't*. I let it drift away as Meg runs her hands up my thighs. For all her angles, she's so much softer than Jafar, her hands smooth where his are rough. I focus on her darkly painted lips and lick my own. She catches the movement and her low laugh has me clenching my thighs. "I think a punishment is in order."

"You took the words right out of my mouth." He pulls my dress up my body and over my head, leaving the stretchy fabric tangled around my wrists on the other side of his head. It's not truly trapping me, but the sensation *feels* like being trapped. Jafar spreads his hand over my lower stomach, forcing me still. "Have a taste, Meg. My baby girl is sweet as fuck."

She parts my pussy with her thumbs and breathes against my clit. "No coming."

"No coming," he confirms.

I can't look away as she closes the last of the distance

between us and gives my clit a teasing lick. Jafar always seems to go down on me like I'm the very air he needs to breathe. Not so with Meg. She tests me with little touches of her tongue, her gaze on my face as if filing away every minute expression.

Jafar chuckles. "So fucking prissy."

"Mmm." She lifts her head but her hand replaces her mouth, stroking me in light touches that curl my toes and have me fighting against Jafar's hold. "How long did it take for her to come the first time? Did you go after her like a starving man?" Her smug smile contains a plethora of knowledge. "Finesse, my friend." She pushes two fingers into me, expertly finding the spot on my inner wall that makes my knees go out.

He adjusts his grip, catching me under my thighs and spreading me wide. Jafar holds me easily, as if he can bear my weight the entirety of the night if he's so inclined. His bruising grip only makes the feeling of Meg's fingers inside me all the hotter. I gasp out a breath. "Daddy, please. Please let me come."

"See." She arches a brow.

"Enough."

I sob out a protest, but Meg gives my pussy one last long kiss and slouches back against the couch. She's left her mark on me in the way of her lipstick, and there's something so obscenely sexy about seeing it smeared across the most private part of me. I want more. I want it now. "Please."

"Ah ah." Jafar sets me back on the ground, yanks my dress off my wrists, and uses a hand on my shoulder to drive me to my knees. "You don't get to tease her and then have us playing with your cunt for the rest of the night. Orgasms are a reward for good girls, and you've hardly been that." He goes to his knees behind me, once again using his body to force mine closer to Meg. "Are you wet, Meg?"

"Always." She laughs. "But if you're asking if that little show got me hot and bothered? Yes, Jafar. I said your baby girl is exquisite and I meant it."

"Take off her pants."

I reach for the front of her slacks with shaking hands. I know what comes next, the same way I know that Jafar wanted me to suck his cock when we played in The Underworld. I'm clumsy working the pants down her hips and off her legs, but it doesn't matter. She's beautiful. A skeleton key is tattooed high on her inner right thigh and a glint of metal piercing near her clit has my mouth watering. "Oh."

It's only when Meg spreads her thighs that I remember I'm supposed to be resisting. I jerk back, but Jafar's presence at my back means I can't go far. "Don't play the innocent now, baby girl. Look at how wet you got her." He reaches around me to wrench Meg's thighs wider.

Her gasp has me shaking. I want her to make that noise again. I want to be the one to cause it.

"Make her come." His command ripples through me, burning through my last facade of resistance. Even as part of me wants to mirror the calculated way she licked me, I'm not capable of that kind of control. I run my palms over her thighs, touching Jafar's hands briefly, and then up her narrow hips to push her shirt up over her breasts. The sight has me clenching my thighs together, and I waste no time dipping down to drag my tongue over her. I work the piercing with my lips, enjoying the contrast of metal and her soft flesh.

Meg lets out a strangled laugh. "She's enthusiastic."

"She's a dirty little slut. She's been fantasizing about getting her mouth all over your pussy from the second you met." Jafar moves back, but I'm too focused on drawing another of those little gasps from Meg to worry about what he's doing behind me. She tastes like sin and I can't get enough. I know I'm in the submissive position, that Jafar—

and to a lesser extent, Meg—are in control, but her thighs tensing beneath my hands because of what *I'm* doing to her sure feels like power to me.

Meg digs her fingers into my hair, pulling me closer yet, guiding my mouth back up to her clit. "Right there." She lets out a little moan. "Don't stop."

It's not enough, though. I want more of her. I push a single finger into her pussy and gasp against her when she clenches around me. *Yes, yes, yes.* I work a second finger into her. "I'm going to make her come, Daddy."

He strokes his hands up my hips, moving back behind me. I freeze. He's removed his clothes while I was busy here. His cock presses against my entrance and I'm wet enough that the tiniest movement on my part would slide him into me. I shouldn't. I *know* I shouldn't, that I am supposed to wait for him to lead, that this is a trap.

It doesn't matter.

I slam back against him, taking his cock deep inside me. My moan turns into a cry of protest when he grabs my hips and forces me off him. "Do you see what I mean? The tiniest taste of cock and she forgets all about her responsibilities and tries to steal an orgasm."

"Naughty girl." Meg tangles her fingers in my hair and pulls me back to her pussy. She tightens her grip at the last second, holding me a bare inch from touching her. "Seems like she deserves a punishment."

"Seems like you're right." Jafar delivers a rough slap to my ass. I whimper even as the heat of the strike zings directly to my clit. "Make her come, baby girl. Don't stop again."

Meg releases my hair and I immediately go back to working her clit exactly like she commanded. Jafar doesn't stop spanking me, the rising tide of pain leaving me desperate. For what, I can't begin to say. His cock. Meg's orgasm. Their hands all over me.

I suck hard on Meg's clit and push two fingers into her. She laughs as she comes, her pussy clenching around my fingers in a way that has me moaning against her. I keep licking her until she pulls me away by my hair. "That's enough." Her laugh is more than a little breathless and a flush has warmed her pale skin. She grins down at me. "That was well done."

Jafar delivers one last slap to my ass and then palms me. "Drenched."

"Of course she is. She loves this." She tugs my hair. "Don't you?"

"Yes," I whisper.

"Look at that, Jafar. Honesty for the first time tonight." Another tug on my hair has me writhing my hips, instinctively trying to ride Jafar's hand even as he removes it. Meg smiles. "Tell us what you want. Be honest."

Somehow, this feels like the most daring thing I've done tonight. I force myself to meet her gaze. Force the truth from my lips. "I want to ride Jafar's cock while you lick my clit and his cock."

If anything, her grin widens. "He's right. You are a dirty little slut." She looks at him. "Shall we give the girl what she wants?"

I nearly topple over as I turn around to face him. As I suspected, he's naked, his body an invitation I can't ignore even if I want to. He pulls me up and takes my mouth, and knowing that he can taste Meg's orgasm on my tongue has me running my hands up his chest and looping them around his neck, pressing my body against him and rolling my hips in invitation. When he finally lifts his head, his dark eyes are so hot, they sear me right to my soul. "If she asks nicely."

"Please, Daddy." I kiss his jaw, his neck, his chest, working my way down to his cock. "Please, please, please." I suck him deep, loving his sharp inhale the same way I loved Meg's moans. More. He laces his fingers through my hair, but for once he doesn't take control, he merely lets me suck him down as I beg without words.

"I'd say she wants it," he rumbles.

"Mmm." I feel Meg shift to the floor behind me before she slides her hand between my legs. "God, she really is drenched, isn't she?" She explores me with her fingers in an absent sort of way, not trying to get me off, just seeming to enjoy touching me.

"Next time, I'm going to bring in a few of the guys." Aside from his voice dropping an octave, I wouldn't know that he's even remotely affected by my mouth around his cock. The fact they're talking about me as if she's not fingering me, as if I'm not sucking him off ... I shiver and tilt my hips a little in invitation.

Meg laughs and pushes two fingers into me. "I saw you talking with Hook while you fingered her. He could barely take his eyes off her and he couldn't even see how wet she was. He'd give his right arm to be able to fuck her pussy while she sucks your cock. Or maybe fuck her pussy while you fuck her ass." She presses her thumb to my ass, the sensation making me moan around Jafar's cock. Meg gives a happy sigh. "I would very much like to watch it when it happens."

"That can be arranged." He uses his grip on my hair to guide me off his cock. "Would you like that, baby girl?"

The thought of two cocks filling me, of being caged in by two bodies, of being helpless and spread wide open ... No question about it. "Yes, Daddy."

"Thought so." He stands and moves back to sit on the chair across from us. "Come on, then."

I scramble to my feet and nearly tip over when my knees try to give out. Jafar catches my hand and pulls me roughly onto his lap. He turns me to face Meg where she still kneels on the floor and uses his legs to spread mine obscenely wide. "I like seeing her lipstick all over your cunt, baby girl."

"Me, too," I whisper.

"Shall we let her get it all over my cock, too?"

"Yes, Daddy."

"Come here, Meg."

I expect her to stand, but she crawls. There is absolutely nothing subservient about the motion. She's lost her shirt somewhere along the way, and Meg puts on a show as she moves slowly toward us. I don't draw a full breath until she's kneeling between our thighs, and then I forget to breathe entirely. She wraps her hand around Jafar's cock, but it's my gaze she meets as she sucks him deep.

One stroke. Two.

Jafar lifts me and Meg moves his cock to my entrance. He slams me down on him and I can't keep a cry inside. I wriggle, trying to adjust to his cock stretching me, but neither of them gives me time. His hands on my hips press me down, sealing us completely, and then Meg's mouth is on my clit. All the finesse is gone. She does something with her tongue that has my vision hazing out. I scream as I come, riding out the long waves of orgasm that never seem to end.

"Meg, enough." At first I think Jafar's warning is about what she's doing to me, but I look down and realize she's cupping his balls and I know without a shadow of a doubt that he's hanging on by a thread.

Meg knows, too, because she doesn't stop. Not what she's doing to me, not what she's doing to him.

"Fucking *enough*." He spills us onto the ground, shoving Meg onto her back and dragging me down her body to push my face against her pussy. "Thank her for that orgasm, baby girl."

He pounds into me as I fuck her with my tongue. I can already feel another orgasm building, but I want her to come again before it happens. I want to feel her unravel and know that I'm the cause. Then her hands are in my hair and she's guiding me back to her clit. I work it just like I did last time, taking her cues to drive her higher.

"Getting distracted, aren't you?" Jafar thrusts deep and slaps my ass. I cry out, desperately licking Meg until she's coming, sucking and licking until she drags me up her body to claim a kiss. Jafar follows until we're straddling her hips.

That's when he begins fucking me in earnest, his strokes going rougher, deeper. Being pinned between their bodies, the slick slide of their skin against mine … Perfection. I cannot put into words how good it is. Meg keeps kissing me and snakes a hand between us to finger my clit. I try to hold out, to make this delirious pleasure last forever, but it's too good. I come, sobbing against her lips. My orgasm tips Jafar over the edge, his strokes going frenzied until he drives deep and curses.

Time moves a little fuzzily after that. Jafar manages to get us both back on the couch and wrapped up in a blanket he pulled out from somewhere. Meg lounges like a jungle cat, all smug satisfaction as she watches me in Jafar's arms. "She's a keeper."

"I'm aware."

She gives one last full body stretch and climbs to her feet. "We should do this again sometime." She pulls on her pants and blouse and slips back into her heels. Meg pauses to press a soft kiss to my forehead. "See you around, Jasmine."

Easy enough to read between the lines.

Remember my offer.

Jafar barely waits for her to leave the room before he stands with me in his arms. "Let's go to bed." He takes me up to the penthouse and straight to his room. A quick shower and then he tucks us up into his bed.

It's so right, so perfect. I want this feeling to last forever. An impossible desire.

Dreams only last until dawn, after all.

CHAPTER 18

JASMINE

I wake up alone. I'm not even surprised when I reach over to find Jafar's spot cold. No doubt he left as soon as I fell asleep, content that he'd fucked me back to submission.

I wish it were the truth.

I wish I could be content in this place he's put me. That I won't constantly look to the sky I'm forbidden. I have been a bird in a cage *my entire life*. Handing me orgasms the way one pacifies a dog with treats isn't enough. Jafar would know that if he wasn't so focused on removing the threat Ali represents. The fact that he doesn't only reinforces the truth—I will always be second to him. No matter what he feels for me, he will pick the territory first every single time.

That's not a reality I can make my peace with.

My decision is jagged glass sitting in my chest, and every move drives the shards deeper. So tempting to lay in his bed all day and wait for him to soothe the feeling with his words and body, demanding submission from me that I'm only too happy to give. I love it, too, after all.

I love *him*.

The realization brings me no joy. If he were another man, if I another woman, then I could luxuriate in this truth. I could take it out and examine it at my leisure and revel in the feeling of being in love with a man like him.

I'm not another woman.

I'm Jasmine Sarraf.

And I am done being a pawn.

I pull up my contacts as I walk back to my room, look at the number I added there after my fitting with Tink yesterday. My thumb hovers over Meg's name. If I do this, there is no going back. Jafar might have feelings for me, but he won't allow that to get in the way of his plans—and his plans include me under this control. He'll attempt to track me down and haul me back to this penthouse the first chance he gets. I hate the thrill that goes through me at the thought. This isn't a game. This is my *life*. I push the button to call.

Meg answers on the second ring. "Good morning, Jasmine. Still thinking about last night?"

I ignore the bolt of heat her words bring. "This is business."

"Ah." The barest of hesitations. When she speaks again, her voice is absent of all emotion. "I take it you've thought about my offer."

The edge of this cliff crumbles beneath my feet. I can't live with myself if I pull back now, if I change my mind and spend the next twenty-five years waffling over my decision. I've already survived that time period under the control of someone else. I can't do it again. I *won't*.

I clear my throat. "I'm going to need assistance getting out of the penthouse."

"Consider it done. Be ready in an hour." She hangs up, leaving me with more questions than reassurances. If she's able to penetrate Jafar's defenses that easily, she must have had this set up already. She was *that* sure of me.

The realization doesn't comfort me, but I doubt anything can at this point. I hurry into my room and pull on a pair of black leggings and a cropped over-sized T-shirt. It's hardly an outfit built for stealth, but it's better than the gowns beginning to clutter up my closet. I pull my hair back from my face and lace up my shiny new tennis shoes.

My phone rings, and I hold my breath as I answer. "Yes?"

"Take the elevator down to the parking garage. Level two."

I don't question Meg. I rush to the elevator and, sure enough, this time it allows me to go all the way down to the indicated level. "Thank you."

"Don't thank me. Like you said—it's business."

As much as I want to argue, I make a noncommittal noise instead. Meg is helping me and that's enough. The reasoning doesn't matter. The actions *do*.

The parking garage is dimmer than I remember it, but it's just as well. A black limousine pulls up and Meg opens the door. There's nothing in her expression to indicate that, fewer than twelve hours ago, I had my face buried in her pussy and licked her to two outstanding orgasms. We might as well be acquaintances for all the warmth she gives me. "Come along."

A small voice chooses that moment to point out that I've done nothing I can't take back yet. Getting into that car crosses a line in the sand, and becomes a betrayal that Jafar will not forgive. If I turn around now, no one has to know what I intended.

I climb into the car.

It's only when the door shuts I realize Meg isn't alone.

Hades smiles at me, the warmth of the expression pushing me back against the seat. Seeing him in the club was one thing, but at least I had Jafar to dampen his presence. I have nothing to shield me now. The man is attractive in a refined kind of way that comes with age and power, his silvered temples and the deep laugh lines bracketing his mouth and eyes marking him as somewhere close to middle age. The black glasses and perfectly tailored suit only add to the impression of a man used to money and comfortable with power. "You've really stirred the hornet's nest, haven't you?"

It's everything I can do not to shrink into myself. There's nothing overtly threatening about this man. Even his question is dry and filled with the amusement Hades seems to give every word that he doles out.

And yet.

The feeling of a threat remains all the same.

I force myself to lift my chin, to meet his dark gaze. "I didn't ask for any of this."

"No, the innocent rarely do." He shrugs as if it's of no concern to him, as if his very presence in this car doesn't represent things I'm afraid to think about.

I glance at Meg. I can't help it. She's perched next to Hades in a short black dress, his hand resting on her thigh with the ease of long familiarity. She doesn't smile or give me any kind of reassurance that I haven't made a terrible mistake, which only confirms that I have.

Damn it, but I should have known better than to expect this gift to come without strings.

I *did* know better, but I ignored my instincts, the prize too tempting to resist.

It takes two tries to clear my throat. "What is it you want?"

"It's not about what I want, sweetheart." He idly strokes Meg's leg. "A man's word is the only thing he has worth anything in this world."

I raise my brows. "I would think the price of your suit and the luxury in your club seems to suggest otherwise."

He chuckles, the sound warm enough that I have to fight not to smile with him. "I do regret that you were pulled into this. You seem like a good girl, and my Meg likes you."

"I do." Meg traces her fingers over the knuckles of Hades's hand. "But, like you said, your word has to mean something."

"Right you are, love." He shrugs. "You seem scrappy. I'm sure you'll come out on top of this."

The car takes a turn and pulls into another parking garage. We've barely been driving ten minutes, if that. I glance out the window as we pull to a stop and go still. Ali stands easily with a pair of men, his gaze hungry as it rests on the car, as if he can see me through the tinted windows. I look back at the couple, at Meg. Is there sympathy in her blue eyes? I can't be sure. "Don't do this. *Please.*"

"Like I said, I'm only as good as my word, and a deal is a deal." He almost—*almost*—sounds sorry about it. I don't believe the regret for a moment, but it's still salt in the wound of betrayal.

I turn to Meg. "Why?"

She has the grace to flush. "He made a deal."

I don't ask what Ali offered them. It doesn't matter. I have to clench my hands to keep from reaching for her, whether in violence or pleading. "What if I want to make a deal?"

"Sorry, love, but he got there first."

Ali wrenches the door open and sticks his head in. He gives Hades a smug grin. "Pleasure doing business with you."

"Wish I could say the same." He waves his hand. "Take your woman. I expect you to follow through on the terms within the week."

"Consider it done." Ali grabs my hair and half drags me out of the car, dropping me at his feet. He slams the door shut and stands over me, seeming to relish the position. "Hello, Jasmine."

I gingerly touch my stinging scalp. He made a deal. He's treating me like I'm a cow to be traded, and the derision on his face stings more than my flaming skin. "You bastard."

"Only according to my mother." He laughs, but the men at his back remain as stone-faced as ever. Ali motions to the one on the right. "Pick her up. Let's go."

I don't want to go wherever they intend to take me, but I haven't magically developed combat skills along the way and so I'm helpless to fight as the man ignores my attempts to hit him and tosses me over his shoulder. I barely get a chance to register how different this is than being hauled around by Jafar when the asshole throws me into a trunk. Ali's face is the last thing I see before they slam the lid closed.

A trunk.

That fucker put me *in a trunk*.

Panic flutters in my throat, but I force it down. Jafar might come for me, if only to deprive Ali of his prize, but the fact remains that Ali has evaded Jafar's reach for days. Will he find the man eventually? Yes, I have no doubt of it. Will he find him in time to save me?

That, I can't guarantee.

I close my eyes and concentrate on taking slow breaths until I can think clearly again. I can't count on help, which means I must save myself. The path forward isn't clear to me, but there's not a single thing I can do while I'm trapped in a trunk. I *cannot* panic. Panic is death.

I settle in to wait.

Time passes strangely without any indicators to guide me. It could be fifteen minutes before the car rolls to a stop. It could be two hours. Despite my best intentions, I'm left blinking stupidly into the light when Ali opens the trunk and grins down at me. "Welcome home, Jasmine."

Horror washes over me with a sickening finality. Surely he can't mean …

But when he pulls me to my feet, I see that he meant it in the most literal way possible. He's brought me back to my father's house. My legs refuse to hold me, but that barely causes Ali to blink. He merely motions to his man to pick me up again. There's no crowd waiting for us this time, just an eerie echoing feeling that makes me believe everyone else has emptied out. And why not? This house makes little sense as a location for a base of operations. It's not even in the city proper. Of course Jafar would have ordered the men to move to key spots in his territory to consolidate power.

Has he even been back here since that night?

They carry me down the hallway, and I stare hard at the spot where Jafar fucked me. My panties and robe are still wadded up against the wall, evidence of what I considered my shame. The very idea is laughable now. That night was the cumulation of five years of stifled desire and need. I still desire Jafar. My leaving changed nothing.

I can't rely on him to save me.

Ali's man drops me to my feet and Ali grabs my arm in a rough grip to shove me into an all too familiar room. *My* room. He stalks to the wall and yanks the landline phone out of the wall. "You won't be needing that."

I plant my feet and stare him down. "This isn't going to end the way you want it to."

"Bullshit." He hits me. It's almost casual, a backhand to the face that sends me stumbling a few steps from him. The blow is so reminiscent of my father that I laugh. Those are too large of shoes for him to ever be able to fill, even on his best day. Ali is a bully and, if he's sly, he's nowhere near sly enough. Coming back to this house was a mistake, bringing me here an even larger one.

Ali shrugs like he thinks he's some kind of prize fighter. "Play nice, Jasmine, or you won't like what comes next."

I straighten slowly and stare him down. "I suppose we'll see, won't we?"

He must expect me to fall to my knees and beg for mercy, because my calm seems to rattle him. Ali shakes his head. "I'll come for you later." And then he's gone, sweeping out of the room and slamming the door behind him. I listen and, sure enough, the lock clicks as he seals me in. It seems I am forever destined to be locked away by men.

No longer.

I cross to my desk, to the spot on the floor where, half hidden by my rug, my sharp letter opener lays where it fell that first night. I hesitated then, whether because of nerves or because some part of me recognized the man in my room as Jafar.

I won't hesitate again.

The letter opener feels good against my palm, its cool a contrast to the angry heat throbbing in my cheek where Ali hit me. A feeling wells up inside me, the sensation akin to seeing a train barreling down the tracks in my direction. I could try to flee, but the train is inside me. There is no escape. Instead I welcome it with open arms, embracing the emotion fully and letting it permeate every part of me.

Rage.

It's blades and fire and pain, twenty-five years cumulation of it. How many times have I swallowed this emotion down, again and again until I'd surely choke? So many nights spent staring into the darkness and wondering if it mirrored what I held inside me.

Now I know the truth.

I take a breath, and then another, forcing air into my lungs. Rage is only useful if it doesn't hamper my ability to think and plan. I glance at the door. Ali will come for me. If not today, then tonight. He can't cement his power grab without appearing to bring me to heel, just like Jafar needed the appearance of doing the same.

Always the pawn and never the queen.

Fuck. That.

I'm taking the throne now, and if I have to cut Ali to pieces in the process, he deserves nothing less. In fact, I welcome the violence. I take a step toward the door before I catch myself and turn to the desk. I may have learned to pick the lock of my bedroom door when I was all of seven years old, but walking out of this room without a plan is foolish in the extreme. That's the rage talking, and I need logic to guide my steps, even if the anger is what will give me the strength to do what needs to be done.

The strength to kill Ali.

CHAPTER 19

JAFAR

"She's gone."

After last night, I spent all day waiting for this call. Knowing what we shared wasn't enough to keep Jasmine at my side.

I pinch the bridge of my nose. "Keep a man on her for the time being." As tempting as it is to track Jasmine down and haul her ass back to the penthouse, if I do that, I'll break something between us. Something new and fragile and infinitely rarer than I could have dreamed.

I love her.

The truth should be cause for celebration. She loves me, too. She might not have said it aloud, but it's there in the trust she places in me every time we interact. Relationships have been started on less, and ours has a whole hell of a lot of foundation—and baggage. It's the latter that we have to work through, and right now that means Jasmine needs her space. When I put her in the penthouse, I wondered how long it would take her to figure out how to override the elevators. Her father tried to lock her up, too, but she always managed to slip free of the barriers he put in place. A locked door had nothing on that woman.

Yes, I love her, and that means I have to let her go.

Jeremiah clears his throat. "Sorry, Jafar, I wasn't clear. Someone outside hacked the elevators to take her down to the parking garage. I have her getting into a car I've traced back to The Underworld."

I go still. "Did she make a deal?" It's more rhetorical question than anything, but Jeremiah answers me all the same.

"I don't think so. It took us a few minutes before we realized she'd left the building, but they didn't go straight back to the club. They took a detour to a hotel around the corner." A hesitation, the only warning I get before he delivers unwelcome news. "They dropped her there. With Ali."

My vision goes white for several seconds and it's all I can do to breathe through the fury. "Then Ali is the one who made the deal."

"That's my bet."

I turn and head for the exit. It's one thing for my woman to decide she needs some fucking space and take it. This isn't that. Jasmine would never go to Ali, not willingly. If that was even an option, she wouldn't have begged me to save her that first night. She wouldn't have vomited after her encounter with him in The Underworld. To think of her in his hands right now …

I can't afford to think about it. "Find him, Jeremiah. If he was in that hotel, then he left record. Find him right fucking now."

"Yes, sir."

I hang up and stare at the phone clenched in my hand. As satisfying as it would be to shatter it, it's not worth the outward expulsion of anger. I close my eyes and count to ten, and then I do it a second time. My fury hasn't retreated, the sharp edge of fear driving it on, but I can think clearer now.

Jeremiah might be able to track Ali down now that we have an active starting point, but I know someone who will have that information at hand.

Hades was never one to leave anything up to chance.

I almost order my men to the car, but if my arrival appears like I'm launching an attack, that's exactly how Hades will respond. The Underworld has only been under siege once before. It was before my time, but word has it that it lasted over a month before some sort of agreement was put in place. Jasmine doesn't have thirty days.

She might not have even one.

It takes me twenty minutes to reach the club. I can barely hold myself still as I take the elevators up. I have never had a problem containing my emotions when my goal was at hand. Emotion is something to manipulate in other people. Letting it get the best of me? Unacceptable.

That's not an option right now.

I keep thinking of the fear on Jasmine's face that morning at The Underworld. The way she was willing to move to violence the night her father sold her in marriage to Ali. He will break her. I wasn't lying when I told her that. I'm a monster, but at least I admit as much from the start. Ali plays the part of a hero, a good guy, and saves his dark deeds for private.

Meg meets me at the second set of elevators. She holds up her hands. "You do not want to go up there looking like that."

I plant my feet because I don't trust myself to get close to her, not with Jasmine's life and safety on the line. "You were there last night. You're the one who put this into motion."

She narrows her eyes. "Don't try the white hat card, Jafar. Not with *me*. We're all playing our own games right now. I'm sorry Jasmine got caught up in them, but it changes nothing."

I glance up, as if I can concentrate hard enough to see

through the floor to where Hades is no doubt holed up. "He took that deal knowing it would cross me."

"He takes a lot of deals knowing they will cross a lot of people. Don't act like you're special."

"She considered you a friend."

"Did she?" Meg raises her brows. "Then you should thank me for removing her from your care because she's a goddamn liability."

I hate her in that moment. Meg pretends she's above us baser creatures, but the truth is that she's right down in the muck with us. If she wanted out, she could have pulled it off years ago. "If something happens to her because of his deal, I'll personally burn this place to the ground."

"You'll try." She gives me a long look. "You care about her."

"No shit I care about her. Fuck, Meg, did you think this was all about power?"

"Power and sex." She shrugs and toys with her long brown hair. "It always was for you."

"It's not so simple. Not with her." I lose my cool and rake my fingers through my hair. This was a wasted trip. Once Hades makes a deal, he never goes back on it. He could give me the information I need if he's feeling generous, but Meg standing here, playing the part of gatekeeper means that's not the case. "Where is she?"

"Jafar." She shakes her head slowly. "You know better. The deal was made. We've washed our hands of the situation until it's time to collect payment."

I bite back my snarl at last minute. "Then I'm wasting my time."

"Yes, you are." She turns and walks to the elevators. She doesn't look back.

I misplayed this from the beginning. I was so determined not to owe anyone anything that I didn't even consider taking one of Hades's deals. The second I realized Ali was gunning for Jasmine, I should have done whatever it took to remove him. Now she's paying for my arrogance.

Fuck.

There's nothing to do but leave. I take the elevators back down to the ground floor. I'm pulling out my phone as I catch a flash of green from the corner of my eye. I look up as Tink approaches, her expression just as irritated as ever. She shoves a piece of paper at me. "Get her back, asshole." And then she's gone, striding into the elevator and jamming the button to close it.

I carefully unfold the paper and hiss out a breath. I recognize Hades's artful handwriting. That shit is almost calligraphy. The note is short and to the point.

Balthazar's house.

This balances the scales.

-H

Balances the scales. I take a slow breath. If Ali hadn't trespassed in The Underworld and pissed Hades off, I'd be shit out of luck right now. I can't think about that too closely, can't consider how narrowly this edged in my favor.

I dial Jeremiah. "Stop what you're doing and get all the men. I know where they are."

It was time to get my woman.

CHAPTER 20

JASMINE

*A*li requests my presence at dinner. I might laugh at the farce of normality if I had the ability to laugh right now. Instead, I'm sitting across the table from my enemy in a white gown with a letter opener up my sleeve. Not close enough to strike. Not yet.

I listen with half an ear as he goes on and on about how clever he is for outmaneuvering Jafar for this long. About how sorry he is that my father paid the price of Jafar's betrayal. How happy he is to save me from the enemy. On and on, until I want to clamp my hands over my ears and scream just to drown out his charming voice. It doesn't matter how many words he spills into my silence; he can't alter the truth.

Jafar may be the villain of this piece, but he's not the only one—or even the worst.

I drink my white wine and keep my expression blank. His two men, the only two I've seen since we arrived, hold positions on either side of the door to the hallway. Too far away to stop me from using my blade, but then I'm too far away right now, too. I realize I recognize one of them. He's one of my father's men, though his name dances on the tip of my tongue. My father wasn't a fan of encouraging anything resembling familiarity with his daughter, something that will work against me now. This man backing Ali doesn't bode well for him switching sides to support me.

There is no right time for this. The hungry way Ali watches me tells me everything I need to know. He'll try something tonight, likely right after dinner. If I'm smart, I'll wait for us to be alone to make my move. Surely he won't have his men watch him try to take me. I don't know, and because I don't know, I can't risk it.

That's not the only reason, though.

Always a pawn, but never a queen.

That's how I've considered myself since the beginning. If I want to change that, *truly* change that, then it has to be public and it has to send a statement that cannot be refuted. I close my eyes and fling a prayer into the universe. I'm not sure I believe in a higher power, but if one exists, if it's listening, I can use all the help I can get for what comes next.

"You're not even paying attention," Ali snarls.

I open my eyes and wrestle my expression into something resembling a smile. "Of course I am."

He snaps his fingers. "Come here, Jasmine." His slow grin makes my stomach clench in revulsion. "I haven't gotten a look at you in that dress I bought you." He waits for me to obey, to push to my feet and round the table to stand before him. The dress is fine, if not something I would choose for myself. It hugs my breasts and stomach before flaring out at the hips and falling in a wave to the floor. The high collar might have given it the illusion of modesty if not for the way the fabric clings to my body. I forewent a bra and the way Ali's gaze zeroes in on my chest is the reason why. If he's so focused on my breasts, he won't be watching my wrists.

"Do you know why I chose white?"

Pretending to be interested in this conversation makes me sick, but I manage to keep the emotion from my tone. "Why did you choose white?"

"Because it's our wedding day, Jasmine."

That stops me short. I finally look at him, *really* look at him. "I'm not marrying you, Ali. I was never going to."

His easy smile remains in place, but his dark eyes flare with anger. "That's where you're wrong. You're bought and paid for. Whether or not your father lived long enough to enjoy the riches doesn't change the fact that you're mine by contract. Desire has nothing to do with it, but," He gives me another long look. "It doesn't hurt that you're beautiful."

My rage rises again, so strong it steals my breath from my lungs. I glide a step closer to him. Almost within reach now. "Beautiful, yes. Rich, too, once you reclaim my father's assets from Jafar." I almost, *almost* stumble over his name.

"You're a prize. There's no doubt about that." He holds out a hand. "Come here."

I place my left hand in his and allow him to pull me close to stand between his thighs. Ali isn't particularly large, but he's strong. Stronger than I am, at least. I will my body soft and pliant. "You want to get a look at what you purchased."

"Can you blame me?" He keeps a grip on my wrist and runs his free hand over me. My stomach. My breasts. My pussy. The way I imagine a man examining a horse for purchase might. There's no heat in his touch, but that doesn't stop me from fighting not to be sick. Finally, Ali sits back, his expression contemplative. "Definitely a prize."

I search for words, but I have nothing except rage. "Ali?"

"Yeah?"

I lean down slowly, my gaze fastened to his mouth. I pretend he's another man, one with a close beard and wickedly curved lips. Jafar. No, I can't think of him. Not in this moment. I tug on my wrist, and he releases me so I can run my thumb along his bottom lip. "Can I tell you something I've never told another person?"

"What's that?" His gaze goes a little hazy as I shift closer to straddle him. I *have* to be close for this to work. I have to be able to strike before he can counter.

I lean down until I'm sure he can feel my breath against his lips. "I would rather die than let you fuck me." I jam my blade into his throat and wrench with all my strength. He shoves me away, but it's too late. We're both covered in blood. His blood. I straighten and force myself to watch as the life flees his dark eyes. I did this. I chose this. I will bear witness.

I lift my blade as the two men reach his body. "You have a choice right now, gentlemen. You can bend a knee or you can join him."

"You *bitch*." The stranger starts for me, violence in his gaze.

He makes it two steps before my father's man shoots him in the back. We watch him sink to the ground and then I turn my attention to Jonah. That's his name. I raise my eyebrows, determined not to show the fear slithering through me. "You have something to say, Jonah?"

He slides his gun back into his shoulder holster and considers me. "Your father saw you as a daughter, rather than a person." When I simply wait, he continues. "You've proven that you're his heir in every way that counts." He nods at Ali's body. "Not everyone will follow you, but enough of us will."

This is what power feels like. The heady sensation leaves me dizzy and breathless, but I let none of it filter through to my expression. I glance down at my dress. Red paints the front and soaks the hem. As much as I want to rip it from my body, it sends a message I would be foolish not to utilize.

"Gather them." I absently clean my blade on the dress and roll my shoulders. "The foyer."

"Yes, ma'am."

It's only when he's gone that I consider this could be a trap. But to what end? Jonah could have just as easily attempted to do what both Jafar and Ali did—use me to send his shooting star right to the top of the hierarchy. It might even work. It seemed to well enough for the others.

If it's *not* a trap?

Perhaps there are those who don't want to rock the boat. Who were pleased with the way of things before Jafar's coup and would be just as happy to go back to that at the earliest opportunity. I can't blame them for the desire, for wanting to throw their lot in with the person they believe will make that happen.

I make my way slowly to the foyer. My dress leaves red marks on the tile behind me, which is a mood all on its own. I keep my chin up and shoulders back, even when faced with twenty men, each of which could kill me with the brush of a finger against a trigger. No one looks particularly aggressive, but it's up to me to ensure things stay that way.

They part to allow me through to the stairs, and I feel their attention like a physical weight against my skin. So much expectation, and I'll only have one shot to convince them I can deliver. I take a shallow breath and project my voice. "I am my father's daughter." The truth, even if it sits ill in my chest. "We have had pretender after pretender attempt to use me to cement your loyalty." The thought of Jafar almost stops me cold. He'll never forgive me for this, for snatching this power right out from underneath him. This operation was something he'd planned on since he took the position with my father, and now I'm placing myself squarely between him and his ambition, forcing him to choose.

I'm not sorry.

I love him. I think he loves me, too. But if there's one thing Jafar worships in this life, it's power. How can love compare to that kind of devotion?

"Swear fealty or get out. This will be your only chance. Insubordination will not be tolerated." I spread my hands, knowing all too well the picture I paint. The bloody bride, who will murder any man who tries to bend her to his will. "You know the price of disobedience. Decide now."

One man turns and walks out. I recognize the one who wanted Jafar to *share* me that first night. I wait, but no one follows him. It's better than I dared hope. I nod to Jonah. "Bring in the ones who scattered at my father's death. Give them the same choice, and respect it." I turn my attention to the rest of them. "Set up a perimeter. We will have to retake several of the facilities, but you're more than up to the task. Reclaiming my father's legacy starts now." The words taste foul on my tongue, but it's a sentiment these men can understand. Can respect.

I turn and walk slowly up the stairs. This might have been the first sticking point, but it will not be the last. Others will test me and I'll have to put them down in order to prevent a full-scale rebellion. I clench the skirt of my dress with shaking hands to hide even that small tell. I'll get through it. I don't have any other choice.

It's only when I've locked myself in my room, stripped out of the hated dress, and stepped beneath the scalding hot water that I allow the tears to fall. I didn't want this. Any of it. Not my father's legacy, not the price it will demand of me.

But it's the cost of my freedom. To be answerable to no one but myself means stepping from my father's shadow—from Jafar's shadow, from Ali's shadow—and into the role of queen.

I watch the water run pink and press my lips together to keep the sobs internal. Had I thought Jafar and I stood a chance, even after I left him? He'll come for me. I have no doubts about that.

But will he bend a knee?

Or will I lose him forever?

$\mathcal{W}$e make it to Balthazar's house in record time, and even then I know it's not fast enough. Hours have passed since Ali took Jasmine, hours in which he could have done anything to her. He won't have killed her, but that is the *only* thing I can guarantee. Next to me, Jeremiah keeps a white-knuckled grip on the steering wheel as we take the winding curves leading to the house at reckless speed. I can't relax, can't affect an unconcerned tone. My ability to dissemble has disappeared alongside Jasmine. "We do nothing to jeopardize her safety."

He clears his throat. "That puts us at a disadvantage if he starts shooting the second we pull up to the house."

"*Nothing*, Jeremiah. That's an order."

It takes five minutes longer to reach the gate, and I spend the entirety of that time going over the different choices I could have made to prevent Jasmine from feeling like she had to run from me. Fuck, how many times did I offer to get her out? Rationally, I know that my giving her an out isn't the same as her taking one for herself, but fear surpasses logic time and time again.

She's in danger.

She's suffering at Ali's hands *right now*.

It's my fault.

We stop in front of the gates, the trio of cars behind us falling in line. It's closed, barring access to the property, but I expected no less. What I didn't expect is Balthazar's former head of security standing there with his arms crossed, his gun on full display. He didn't make the jump with me, and last I heard, he wasn't exactly pleased with Ali either.

Why the fuck is *he* here?

I ignore Jeremiah's noise of warning and climb out of the car. I round the front, but stop several yards away. "I'm here for Jasmine."

Jonah shakes his head slowly. "You made that play, and it was the wrong one."

"What the fuck are you talking about? Ali is making the same play."

"Was."

I narrow my eyes. "What's that supposed to mean?"

"Exactly what I said." Jonah is as implacable as ever. "Get back in your car. If she wants to see you, you can go through —just you and whoever is in the first car. The others will wait."

I try to pick his words apart. Ali was making the same play, past tense. If *she* wants to see me? What the hell is going on? I barely smother my need to pepper Jonah with more questions. He won't answer me, and it might piss him off enough to refuse us access. We can fight our way through the gate if we have to, but if there's a chance to get through on peaceful terms, I have to take it. "So be it."

I walk back to the car and climb inside. "Tell the others to wait here."

Jeremiah gives me a look like I've lost my damn mind.

Maybe I have. He finally says, "Are you sure that's a good idea?"

"No. But it's the only option we have."

Several long minutes later, the gates open and Jonah motions us forward. I find myself holding my breath, but I can't stop. I dread whatever we'll find in the massive sprawling house. I should have protected Jasmine. My failure put her in this position, and there isn't a damn thing I can do to earn her forgiveness. I have to make my peace with that, with the knowledge that I'll mow down anyone who lays a hand on her. At least then I'll know she's safe.

Even if she's no longer mine.

My chest feels too tight as we stop near the front door and head inside. With only Jeremiah as backup, I should be more concerned with my own skin. He's good, but no one is *that* good. I'm not. My world has boiled itself down to the necessities. Two words.

Find. Jasmine.

It turns out I don't have to look hard. She's coming down the staircase, her hair pulled back into a braid, a bruise blossoming across the right side of her face. Her dress is the color of life's blood, a red so dark it's almost black, and it flares around her with every step. A glint of metal in her hand forms into the same blade she threatened me with the first night.

This is not a victim rushing to meet her savior.

This is a queen considering whether or not to treat with an enemy.

She stops halfway down the steps, and though I'm conscious of men filtering into the room around us, I can't take my eyes off her. "Ba—Jasmine."

"Jafar." Even her voice sounds stronger, fiercer. As if she's found her footing and she no longer needs my assistance to stand tall. She studies me for a long moment. "Ali tried to take something I wasn't willing to give, and he's dead because of it."

Ali is dead.

I don't have to read between the lines to know that my baby girl killed him, likely with that knife she's clinging so tightly to. Fuck, but I would have saved her from that if I could. Even though I try to moderate my tone, my next words come out low and ragged. "I'm sorry."

She lifts the knife to examine, the blade glinting in the light. "I've decided that I'm done being a pawn. My father may not have considered me his heir, but I *am* his heir in truth. His men—*my* men—have accepted that. The only question remains is whether you will bend the knee and come back into the fold, or if it's exile."

Exile.

She's not bluffing. If I can't accept her as queen, if I try to force her back into the box she's lived in for her whole life, then she'll drive me out. It might break her heart to do it, but she loves her freedom more than she cares about me.

I don't fault her for it.

How can I?

No, pledging myself to another ruler was never part of my plan. If someone asked me yesterday if I'd consider it, I would have laughed them out of the room. But this isn't just another ruler. This is Jasmine. If I cling to my pride, I will lose her, and my instincts say I won't get another chance. This isn't something I can override with lust and dominance to get her to bend to my will. She's drawn a line in the sand and I can step to it or I can get the fuck out.

In the end, it's no choice at all. Not when I can still taste the fear and desperation at the back of my throat. The certainty that I'd lost her forever. What is a kingdom without a queen? I always intended for her to be by my side. It may not have looked like *this*, but does it matter? I'll have the territory, and I'll have Jasmine, too.

Not as a submissive.

As a full partner.

Slowly, so slowly, I go to one knee at the bottom of the stairs. "My queen." I can feel Jeremiah behind me following my motion, repeating my words.

Jasmine nods slowly. "Good." She shifts her gaze to Jeremiah. "Inform the rest of his men. Jafar, with me." She turns and starts back up the stairs.

I follow, matching her pace and maintaining the distance between us. Unexpected pride warms me, pulling at the edges of my lips. Damn, but she never ceases to surprise me. In all the scenarios I tortured myself with on the trip from the city to this place, I never once considered that she would turn the tables on Ali, that she would step into a leadership role and claim it as her rightful place as heir. More the fool I am. Ali underestimated her, but I have, too. Something I suspect I'll be making up to her for a long time.

If she'll allow it.

She leads the way to her room. I close the door softly behind us and wait. As much as I want to go to her, to run my hands over her body to ensure she's not hiding more injuries, to demand answers I don't have the right to.

Really, there's only one thing to say. "I'm sorry."

Jasmine sets her knife on the desk and turns to face me. "I killed Ali."

"I'm sorry," I say again. "You shouldn't have had to do that." I should have handled it before he ever got close enough to become a danger to her.

"He didn't get a chance to hurt me." She absently touches her face. "Except for this."

I want to bring that fool back from the dead and kill him again for laying a hand on her. Saying so won't do a damn thing but cloud the room with my anger. "You took your father's place."

"Yes. I did."

I hate this. We've been many things with each other, but never stilted and unsure. I run my hands through my hair. "I'll honor my pledge, Jasmine. You have no reason to trust that, but I will."

"I know." She fists the fabric of her dress and seems to force herself to relax. Finally, she lifts her chin and pins me with a fierce look. "I'll be your equal, or I'll be nothing. Do you understand me? Just because I love you doesn't mean that I will sit at your feet ever again." The slightest of hesitations. "At least not outside of the privacy of our bedroom."

Something like hope flares in my chest, the sweep of it through my body leaving me dizzy. "You love me."

"Of course I love you, you fool." She takes a step and then another, moving slowly to place her hands on my chest. "I understand what you were trying to do with me, but I can't live on someone else's terms any longer. I have to fly or dash myself on the rocks below, but it has to be *my* choice. Can you live with that?"

I reach up and run my finger along her jaw, careful to avoid the bruise. "Out there, I'll be your right hand."

"Yes." No hesitation. Just a calm agreement.

"In here?"

She smiles slowly. "In here, I'm your baby girl." The smile fades. "Can you live with that?" she asks again.

"Marry me."

Jasmine leans into my touch. "Ask me again in a year, when I've solidified my place at the head of this beast. Then we'll see." It's not a yes, but I'm strangely okay with that. Even if she never wears my ring on her finger, she's mine in every way that counts.

And I'm hers.

In the end, there's only one answer. "Yes, I can live with that. As long as I have you, I can live with a whole hell of a lot."

She exhales slowly, as if part of her doubted my answer. Jasmine takes a step back and then another. "Then we should celebrate." She lifts an eyebrow, the mischief in her dark eyes a balm to my soul. This woman sees me in a way no one ever has before. She *challenges* me in a way no one has before. I lean forward as if I can catch the words as soon as they fall from her lips. Jasmine smiles. "You asked me how many times I fantasized about you over the years."

"I did."

"I've always wanted you to fuck me in this bed." She takes another step back until she hits the mattress, her smile widening. "Fuck me, Daddy. Make it better than I could have imagined."

I take a step toward her and she meets me halfway, crashing into me as if she needs the reaffirmation as much as I do. I rip her dress off her and curse when I find her naked beneath it. "Always asking for it."

"I knew you'd come for me." She kisses my neck, my jaw, my mouth. "I wanted to be ready for you when you walked through the door."

As if she never doubted me, never doubted that I'd do whatever it took to stand at her side, to be with her. Her faith humbles me even as it drives my frenzy for her higher. I lift her and she instantly wraps her legs around my waist. The bed is too far away. I need to be inside her now, to cement this new future between us. To bolster it.

Jasmine must feel the same way. She reaches between us, trusting me to hold her up, and frees my cock. A breath later and she has me at her entrance. I thrust into her in a single smooth motion, the perfection of the moment nearly sending me to my knees. "I love you, baby girl."

"I love you, too, Daddy." She kisses me. Fuck, but I could lose myself in Jasmine's taste, in the way she strokes her tongue against mine, claiming me even as I claim her.

Perfection.

I bear her down to the bed. "Better be quiet. You wouldn't want your men to hear you coming around my cock."

"That's right. *My* men." She digs her heels into the small of my back, driving me to fuck her harder. Her breasts bounce with each stroke, and her expression is so fucking fierce. "Cover my mouth. Make me come, Daddy."

Pressure is already building in my spine, this mutual claiming too fucking sexy to hold out for much longer. "You're the queen. Make yourself come."

Her smile damn near blinds me. She hooks the back of my neck and drags my mouth down to hers even as she slides her hand between us to finger her clit. She's as primed as I am, and three strokes later, I have to pull back and cover her mouth with my hand as she comes apart around my cock. It's too good. More than that, I *want* to come deep inside her, to seal this new turn in our relationship with something so much stronger than words. I orgasm with a low curse and keep pumping into her, not wanting this to end.

When I finally drop the side of her and hitch her leg over my hip, she laughs. "Why do I have the feeling you're not finished with me?"

"I'll never be finished with you." The truth, stark between us.

Happiness lights up her eyes. "Good." She bites her bottom lip as I push two fingers into her. "I have to meet with my generals in an hour."

"Then we have time for another couple orgasms before you do." I watch her expression go hazy with pleasure, reveling in the fact that it's me here, in her bed, at her side, causing it. "Now that you're queen of your territory, what are you going to do next?"

"You're asking me that *now?*" She laughs breathlessly. "I take it you have a suggestion."

"I do." I push a third finger into her. "Someone recently told me that there's good money and power to be had by taking our operation digital."

"Mmm." She arches into my touch, trying to take me deeper. "This someone sounds rather brilliant."

"She is. Beautiful and brilliant." I dip down to speak directly into her ear. "And mine."

Her hips move as she tries to fuck my fingers. "Say it again."

"Mine." I gather her close, keeping up the touch that will have her coming apart again. "My baby girl, my woman." I nip her bottom lip, catching her cry with my mouth. Only when I've taken her down from the edge do I finish. "My queen."

* * *

THANK you so much for reading Jafar and Jasmine's story! This was a little darker and a little sexier than anything I've written to date, so I hope you enjoyed reading it as much as I enjoyed writing it! If you did, please consider leaving a review.

The Wicked Villains series continues in LEARN MY LESSON, which will feature Hades and Meg as they enact a revenge scheme against a rival's son—Hercules. Except these two sexy powerhouses are *not* prepared to deal with everything Hercules brings to the table. How will they handle him? Join my newsletter to ensure you don't miss the release day announcement!

Want to ensure you never miss a new release or a sale?

Make sure to sign up for my newsletter! Newsletter subscribers also get exclusive content every month, including teasers, cover reveals, and exclusive short stories.

Looking for your next sexy read? You can pick up my MMF ménage THEIRS FOR THE NIGHT, my FREE novella that features an exiled prince, his bodyguard, and the bartender they can't quite manage to leave alone.

* * *

KEEP READING for a look at THEIRS FOR THE NIGHT…

DETERMINED to put it out of her mind, Meg downed her drink and set it on a nearby table. "Let's dance!" She waited for Cara to finish her drink and then towed her friend into the crowd. They carved out a neat little spot for themselves and started moving with the beat. Before long, a guy had grabbed Cara's attention and she was happily grinding on him, stroking his biceps as she spoke in his ear. Meg's laugh was eaten by the music. On her own again, she lifted her arms over her head, tilted her face back and let the strobing lights wash over her.

It was going great until a rough hand closed around her hip and jerked her back into a hard body.

She barely had a chance to register that someone had grabbed her when both hand and body were gone. The absence left her unbalanced and her ankle turned, sending her tipping to the side—right into a large male chest. The stranger caught her easily, his hands cupping her elbows as she found her balance again. Meg looked up…and kept looking up until a pair of devastating blue eyes stole her breath much the same way they had earlier.

The pretty guy from the VIP lounge.

She looked over her shoulder in time to see the other half of the pair dragging a drunk dude through the crowd and toward the exit. *Oh.* One hand released her elbow and gentle fingers clasped her chin, drawing her attention back to her apparent savior.

Not that I needed saving...

He gave a tight smile and mouthed. *You okay?*

How was that even a question? Women got grabbed in clubs all the time. It wasn't okay, but it was hardly worth this level of reaction. Still, it was kind of nice and he was seriously attractive and she found herself nodding slowly.

The second guy returned a few moments later, and Blue Eyes grinned. The expression lit up his face, giving him a playful edge that had her rocking back in her high heels. He leaned down, giving her plenty of time to react, and spoke in her ear. "Dance with us?"

Wait a minute—us?

She angled back enough to look at both of them, at this smiling stranger and his much more serious partner. The vibes coming off the two were so damn strange, Meg didn't know what to do with them, but she found herself nodding as if it was every day that two gorgeous dudes wanted to dance with her at the same time. As if they were a pair and she was...

She didn't know what she was if they were a pair.

They're probably gay, right? This doesn't make sense otherwise.

Straight guys did not share a dance partner the way these two did. They moved seamlessly, transitioning her between them as if they done this a thousand times before. They always seemed to know where the other was, and both kept a careful distance between them and her, touching her only on her hips and nowhere else.

It was so freaking sexy, she could barely stand it.

By the second song, she already had good idea of their

personalities. Blue Eyes seemed to be enjoying himself immensely, always ready with a grin that lit up his expression even as the heat in his gaze damn near melted her panties right off. This one was the kind of guy who threw himself full-tilt into life and to hell with the consequences. His sinful lips promised one hell of a good time and the way he stared at her mouth had her fighting not to lick *her* lips in response.

Dark and Broody was his perfect counterpart. He was bigger than Blue Eyes, his broad shoulders practically blocking out her view of the club. His short black hair was cut serviceably in a way that was just shy of military, and his short beard gave the impression of forgetfulness, rather than following any hipster trend. He wore a plain black T-shirt and jeans, and she would have thought he was just going through the motions except for the fact that he matched his hips to hers with an effortlessness that left her whole body tight. She had no business imaging how he'd use that particular skill in bed and yet…

And yet there was the way he watched her, as if he already knew what she'd taste like and savored the flavor on his tongue like his favorite kind of candy.

The song changed, shifting to one that was on every radio that month and the dance floor surged as people abandoned their drinks and crowded in. The space between Meg and her partners disappeared and she found herself sandwiched between the men. Dark and Broody had his hands on her hips, and she was braced on Blue Eyes's chest. Dark and Broody acted as a wall at her back, keeping the worst of the crowd off them. Blue eyes lifted her hair away from her neck and his lips brushed her ear. "Have a drink with us."

There it was again. That word, ripe with meaning. *Us.*

As if they were a unit and she could take them as one or reject them as one.

Getting ahead of yourself, aren't you? He asked you to have a drink, not to...

The crowd surged again, pressing them ever more tightly together and she froze. There was no mistaking the fact that they wanted her—that they *both* wanted her. Her fingers flexed on Blue Eyes's chest, kneading his pecs, and his hands dropped to her hips, just above where Dark and Broody held her lightly. *His* hands shifted the slightest bit, his pinkies drawing across the bare skin of her thigh just below the hem of her dress. Just that. Nothing more.

But she felt branded right down to her soul.

DOWNLOAD THEIRS FOR THE NIGHT for FREE now!